Click To Subscribe

L.M. Augustine

Chapter 1

Half of the guys in my grade get girls with one flash of a smile. The other 49.999 percent either get straight A's, college scholarships, or a million dollars from their so-rich-they-need-a-personal-chef-even-though-they-always-eat-out parents. And me? I get a camera and a broken heart.

Sunlight warms my back as I push open the front door and reach for my computer. Red and yellow leaves litter the entire front yard, and the poignant smell of autumn is everywhere. I breathe it in, smiling to myself. Everyone knows this is the best season. I mean, winter is all about snow and it's common knowledge that snow stops being cute after the third time shoveling out the driveway. Spring is okay, although I'm mostly in it for the Girl Scout Cookies, and summer is too much fighting over which half-naked girl to flirt with next to be even halfway enjoyable. But autumn is cool, rich, and lively. Autumn is dancing in the leaves with that one person you can't go without.

Autumn is running and jumping in the wind. Autumn is smiling, kissing, loving.

Autumn is happy.

Well, at least it's supposed to be.

Ever since Mom died, though, that whole "happy" thing has been more of a struggle for me than anything else in the world.

With another breath, I log into my computer, click over to my vlog page, and scroll through the fifty-something new comments on my latest video. Most are complimentary, despite the one troll who seems to think my incredibly gorgeous face (my words) is "fat." Honestly, I'm not entirely sure *how* a face can be fat, but okay.

After a quick skim, I already know none of the comments is the one I'm looking for, though.

I started my vlog two and a half years ago as a high school freshman with too much free time and not enough friends to spend it with. Mom used to call it my "imaginary friend" or my "replacement friend," but if that's true, this vlog is one badass imaginary friend. Not too many imaginary friends come with over one-hundred-thousand subscribers.

I check my watch—2:01. *She should be commenting by now.*

She. Harper. The girl who comments every day at exactly 2:02 in the afternoon, and who is one of the few bright spots left in my life. I don't know what she looks like or anything about her, really, aside from our occasional deep philosophical messaging on why pizza tastes so delicious and the fact that she says she lives in the same state as I do. But as stupid as it sounds, I can't stop thinking about her. Can't stop picturing what she looks like, how she smiles, talks, laughs, or even how her lips taste in the moonlight. (I just hope like hell she isn't actually a fifty-year-old man pretending to be a sixteen-year-old girl because talk about awkward.) Sometimes I even wonder what it would be like to see her every day, to have her sit next to me and make fun of me for my taste in cupcakes (pink frosting for the win), to just laugh and talk with her until the world melts away.

I refresh the page and check the time again. 2:02. *Where is her comment?*

It doesn't come until a few seconds later. As a response to my video about love notes in class, "HarperLikesPizza," whose profile is complete with an avatar of a cow riding a bicycle while simultaneously eating pizza, wrote, *"I got a love note once during Spanish class in seventh grade. I'm pretty sure it said I was hotter than a frozen potato."*

I smile to myself. Together, Harper and I are the dorkiest people in existence, and I can't help but love it. It doesn't even matter that her comments are so short. Every interaction with her, no matter how small or pointless, is worth its weight in gold. She could probably lecture me on how a refrigerator works and it still would be awesome.

That's just how she is, though: awesome. Perfect. *Mine.*

I scroll the mouse across the page and click over to message her. A few months back, when our friendship really started to grow and we needed a place to talk outside of comments and emails, Harper and I made this chatroom for each other. Only we have access to it, and it's basically our own little corner of the internet to talk about the history of the tomatoes and not care about the stupidity of it, because we're talking with each other. Sometimes, when I'm bored, I even go back to the chat, reread our conversations, and catch myself smiling at it.

Harper always makes me smile.

Nice, I type. *Being hotter than a frozen potato is pretttty impressive. You deserve some sort of award.*

I know, right?

Plus, it's one hot frozen potato.

So hot it practically burnt the freaking kid's hand, I bet.

Well, it's no wonder with that super sexy new avatar of yours, I type, because I'm smiling just looking at it. Something about a pizza-eating-cow-biker is just so... *her.* I mean, I don't know what she looks like or who she is, but somehow, I still feel like I know her, like we're longtime friends and I don't even realize it. And whoever she is, *wherever* she is, I can't shake off this feeling that she is the one for me.

Yeah. I know. Falling in love with a girl over the internet. Welcome to my effed-up life. (My poor therapist.)

Hey, what can I say? she writes. *My avatar brings all the boys to the yard.*

I stifle a laugh. Oh my god. She is perfect.

Harper commented for the first time on my vlog almost four months ago, and for every week after that, she's kept commenting. Back then, I only liked her platonically. I thought she was just a funny girl on the internet who I enjoyed talking to. Nothing more, nothing less. But slowly, as months passed, I realized I cared about her—like, for real. And at first, that scared the hell out of me.

I bet it's the cow, I say. *Major turn-on if you ask me.*

I knoooow! So what's up with you anyway?

Nothing. Just way too much homework.

SAME!

#awkwardhighschoolsingleprobs

Truth. We're practically *oppressed as a species.*

We should make a club.

I think we already have. Exclusive. Only two people allowed. Just us. One hot potato and one... socially inept video blogger.

I hate you, I type.

I know.

No you don't.

Oh, Sam Green, believe me, I do.

Harper calls me "Sam Green" because that's my vlogging pseudonym, and I still haven't had the guts to tell her my real name. I try to keep my vlog as separate as possible from my real life. My vlog is my happy place; my real life... isn't.

Whatever, I type. I'm fabulous.

You sound like a total diva.

Probably because I am.

Oh yeah? What's your most popular album and how come I've never heard of it?

My album is called "Love Letters To Myself" and you have never heard of it because you were raised poorly and have poor taste in music.

Creative title. And the album cover? Is it a picture of you tossing your hair in the wind?

Obviously. You doubt me?

Of course not.

Sitting on the porch, a slight breeze ruffles my blond hair, and several birds chirp overhead. I glance out at my tightly-packed neighborhood, which is lined with five small houses with even smaller yards per street, and catch myself smiling. When I talk to Harper, all I want is for her to just keep going, for me to keep talking to her, for her to write away the world for me. To make it just us, just me and her.

I'm not sure how one goes about falling in love with a girl over the internet, but I guess I did it pretty freaking easily. One second I thought she was funny and kind of cool and the next I was thinking so much more. I have no idea why I'm so sure about loving Harper, but I just... am. Sure, I could be overestimating this whole thing, but by the deep longing I feel for her every time I'm not back here, talking to her, and by the way I just wish she were closer and closer to me, I don't think so.

Hey, Harper? I type after a while.

Yeah?

Your avatar is sure as hell bringing this boy to the yard.

Chapter 2

When I first started my vlog, it was just another way to pass the time. Back then, I vlogged about high school relationships and also really whatever popped into my head, because let's face it, I am the farthest thing from experienced in the field of relationships. I was bored and I needed a hobby, so I took a deep breath and started filming, thinking I'd just make a few videos and be done with it. But 135,789 subscribers later, it's become a part of me. Vlogging is something I can't *not* to do, and I never feel more at peace than when I'm talking in front of the camera, filming my next vlog. Some nights I stay up thinking about what to vlog about next, while on other nights, I lie awake smiling at the fact that I have, like, *real* subscribers—the one constant in my life nowadays.

I wish I could say vlogging is my whole life, but it's not. It's my safe zone, though—the one thing I can escape to when everything else seems to be falling apart.

As far as I know, no one from my tiny high school, not even Cat Davenport, my best friend, knows about my vlog At least, I have yet to be approached or made fun of for my "loser vlog series," so that's a plus. I vlog under the pseudonym Sam Green for a reason, as this vlog is where I open myself up, and I want it to remain a secret. The only ones who know about it are my mom and me—and that's it. It's weird, how I'm more comfortable being who I really am to complete strangers than to the people I've known all my life. But all the same, it's the truth.

I film my vlogs with the same ritual over and over: I drink a glass of water, take a deep breath, and stare straight into the camera. *You're just talking to Mom*, I remind myself, because I know I can't talk to her any more outside of this, because this vlog is the only way I can feel close to her again. Then, I click play, smile, and begin.

Mom died six months ago, far enough into the past that I should be able to talk about her with a smile, with the months of pain turned to fond memories and rainbows, and her death just another memory.

Keyword: should.

But every morning when I wake to find her gone from the house, it feels like I'm reliving that first day without her over and over again, like I'm trapped in this sub-reality of tears and death and so, so much emptiness. The worst part is I'm not sure I want to leave it, leave her.

I'm not sure I want to let go.

The therapists say it's because of Dad. After all, her whole death *was* his fault. He was wasted one night and decided it was a brilliant idea to drive her home and then… nope. According to the police he was speeding and ran a red light when another car slammed into the passenger door, killing Mom instantly. Dad survived it, even though I wish he hadn't. I mean, I've always hated him, but now? Now he's dead to me. The way I see it, if I can't have Mom, then he can't have me, either.

"West." Cat puts a hand on my shoulder. "You okay?"

"I…" I look up. Her blue eyes lock with mine. "Yeah. I'm okay, I guess," I say.

She rolls her eyes. "You're a terrible liar, you know."

I force a laugh, but it's weighted down by sadness. "Dude, I know."

It's Saturday, and we stand in front of the shopping mall Cat dragged me to (she bribed me with ice cream, naturally) so she could buy what she calls her "new Hogwarts wardrobe," an idea I was immediately intrigued by. I only saw her pick out a wizarding cape of some sort, though, because I was busy hiding in the back of the building behind the sports bras so I wouldn't be seen in a girly clothing store, in a valiant attempt to defend my manhood.

People rush all around here, gossiping and laughing and swinging their shopping bags like weapons in a game of Shopper vs. Shopper. Others shove past us, giving us annoyed looks like we're somehow the cause of their own recklessness. The sun is out, and it's times like these where I'm reminded why a) I hate shopping and b) shopping on a sunny Saturday is the worst idea in the history of ever.

God, that ice cream bribe better be worth it.

"We going?" Cat asks me.

"To get the ice cream?"

Cat nods.

"Hell yes," I say, grinning. "I call a vanilla ice cream with whipped-cream, rainbow sprinkles, chocolate fudge, and a cherry on top."

She rolls her eyes. "Oh god, you're such a four-year-old."

"I believe the appropriate term here is 'hipster.'"

"No. No it isn't."

"Hater."

"Freak."

"Alien child."

She stifles a laugh. "You are also so weird."

"Thank you."

"I meant it as a compliment!"

"Oh," I say, waggling my eyebrow at her. "I know."

She just shakes her head and smiles.

We start walking down the sidewalk, Cat holding her shopping bag full of Harry Potter nerdness and me with my short sleeves and supreme hankering for ice cream. The ice cream shop, of course, is located in the outdoor "kid section" of the shopping mall, wedged right in between the Toys R Us and the tiny Lego store. The crowd quickly thins and soon, parents excluded, we're the only ones older than twelve walking down the sidewalk. I glance at Cat, who only shrugs. We are not ones to fear the judgment of small children.

I met Cat for the first time when I was six. Back then she was still infested with a life-threatening case of cooties and I was familiar enough with the virus to know to keep a safe distance away from her, but even so, I remember finding myself thinking that she was kind of cool, even if being with her could put me at risk for the disease as well. So one day when she was on the swings, I walked up to her, blushing hard. I said hi, and she said hi back, and the next thing I knew I was on the swing next to hers and we were talking about how Nemo and Dory would be so cool to own as fish. I remember us giggling and blushing and smiling our six-year-old smiles that day, and we've been friends ever since. I get her and she gets me and that was always that. Cat is my only real friend, and she's always been there for me when I needed it most. Even after Mom's death, even with Dad's drunken tirades and my total emptiness, she was always there to touch my shoulder and remind me that everything was going to be okay.

And she was right.

Mostly.

We turn the corner, walk a few more steps, and stop in front of a small ice cream shop, *The Icecreamery*, which is filled with flailing children and their grimacing parents. No one even remotely our age is inside, but it's not like we care. The shop is an entirely manly place to eat between its pink exterior, its purple-painted chimney, and the fact that there are crayon drawings all over the inside wall.

Cat turns to me. "Are you ready for the experience of a lifetime?" she says, nodding at the front door.

I grin. "Is Abraham Lincoln dead?"

"Well… there are theories…"

I shoot her a look.

"All right, all right fine…" she murmurs. "We can get your ice cream."

"Good! You ready?"

"Of course."

Then I grab her hand, bellow "ICE CREAM!" and we charge, laughing, into the store. A small bell rings as soon as we enter, as if to say "welcome to heaven," and proceeds to blast us with cool air and the squeals of small children all around. The door shuts behind us, and Cat and I pant, grinning at each other. I try to ignore the weird looks of parents as I approach the glowing ice cream freezer.

The cashier gives a little smile, clearly recognizing us from the hundreds of other times we've been there. "You again," she says as I place my hands on the counter like I own the place.

"Us again," I reply. "Good to see you, Sharon."

She rolls her eyes. "Didn't I tell you not to call me that?"

"You did."

"I could kick you out for disrespecting me."

"But you won't for the simple reasons that I am your favorite customer and also, that I am just wonderful."

Sharon turns to Cat, who gives her a sympathizing look. "I'll serve you first, this time," Sharon says to Cat. "I like you better anyway."

I feign a horrified gasp, and Cat elbows me in the side. "I'm glad you've come to your senses. I'd like a scoop of your finest vanilla ice cream," she says way too seriously, holding her head up high. "In

a kiddy cone, preferably. Also with rainbow sprinkles."

Then Sharon turns to me, a smile flickering across her lips,

enjoying torturing me. Neither of them seems to understand just how

intimate my relationship with ice cream is.

"I'll have the same," I say.

Sharon nods, turns to the freezer, and when she brings us

back our ice cream we pay her and sit down in the corner of the ice

cream shop, our cones in hand. For a long moment, Cat and I just

stare, eyes flickering between each other and our respective ice

creams.

"Are you ready, Cat Davenport?" I say.

"Wait…" Cat scoots in her chair and leans forward into her ice

cream. Then she gives a slight nod, and the ritual has begun. "Ready,"

she says.

I lean forward. "Goooood. Race to see who finishes their ice cream first?"

"Of course."

"Winner buys the other ice cream next time?"

"Again, of course." She takes a breath. "On your mark," Cat says and smiles.

"Get set," I say and smile along with her.

"GO!" we shout at once.

Then, we both jump forward and shove our ice creams into our mouths. I attack mine one giant bite at a time, ripping the cone in half and ignoring the rainbow sprinkle casualties. I eat way too fast, vanilla ice cream flying everywhere (and let me tell you: it is one *hell* of an ice cream.) I glance up at Cat, whose cone is down to about half. I rush to eat more but before I can, she devours the entire thing in a bite. I stare at her in horror.

She just shrugs. "I win," she says.

"Unfortunately."

"Unfortunately?"

"You heard me, Davenport," I say, and finish my ice cream. The "loser's bite," we call it.

When I'm done eating, Cat and I move on to laughing about random things and, of course, trash talking each other in preparation for the next ice cream contest. Cat has vanilla all over her mouth and I'm sure I do too, but I don't think either of us even cares.

"I change my mind," Cat says. "*We* are so weird."

"It's pretttty freaking awesome. You know, being weird," I say.

"It is."

I wipe my mouth with the napkin. "So are you going to tell me about your Harry Potter apparel?"

"You mean my Hogwarts wardrobe?"

"Sure?"

"Oh, well, it's nothing vital. Just a new line of nerd fashion that's going to alter the lives of Harry Potter fans across the globe. NBD." She says it all so blankly that I can't help but laugh.

"Wow. That sounds bleak."

"Also, with these new clothes, I'm probably going to attract some paparazzi and everyone is going to want to be me because of how incredibly hot I look. So, the usual. You wouldn't understand," she adds.

"I wouldn't?"

"Oh yeah. You just don't know what it's like to be awesome."

I toss my hair. "Bitch, I'm fabulous."

I catch her stifling a giggle, which makes me smile, too.

"Sure thing, West. Sure thing. All the girls flock around you on your way to your kiddy ice cream shop, too, am I right?"

"Yep. They cling to my killer biceps the whole time."

"I can't even picture that."

I shrug. "It's only the natural reaction when you see a hot guy walking down the street."

"No, I mean I can't picture *you* having *biceps*."

At that, I stick out my tongue at her like a true adult. "Okay. Fine. You got me there, Davenport."

"I totally did."

There's a pause, and my gaze wanders to the scribbled-on white wall in front of me as I listen to the squeals of the kids and the methodic shushing of their parents. Surrounded by the smell of ice cream and the cool air of *The Icecreamery*, I realize once again how glad I am to have Cat and these Ice Cream Saturdays. Anything to keep me from being cooped up at home with my dad, with only my camera to escape to, is more than welcome.

I turn to Cat after another minute, opening my mouth to say something about her Harry Potter wardrobe, but I close it when I notice a sliver of vanilla ice cream still on her lips. "Oh," I say, and I reach for my napkin. "I think you got something there…"Without even thinking, I grab the napkin, lean forward, press it to her lips, and gently dab the ice cream off. "There," I murmur, and sit back down, the warmth of her lips seeping through the napkin and tickling, almost tempting, my fingers. "All better."

It takes me a moment to realize how tense Cat's body suddenly is, how she's staring at me with those wide blue eyes of hers, a mix of alarm and a faint hint of curiosity on her face. My stomach drops, and I feel my muscles freeze, too. Shit. Did I do something wrong? Shit shit shit.

My whole face flushes when I realize she's tensing over the napkin. Oh god, was that wrong? Too far? Too overfriendly? I wasn't even thinking when I did it, I just assumed it would help and then… boom.

"I... um... am sorry," I mutter and snap my gaze back down to my feet. I can't help but notice how the warmth of her lips lingers on my fingertips. "I didn't mean it like that, I just wanted to help..."

"It's nothing," she says quickly. "I was just surprised... is all. Yeah," she says, nodding to herself. "Surprised. That's it."

"So, how was the ice cream?" I say after another instant of us both blushing and not meeting each other's gazes, changing the subject immediately.

She takes a deep breath, closes her eyes, and her face goes back to normal like nothing ever happened. She proceeds to look at me like I'm an idiot. "West," Cat says. "It's ice cream. What do you think my answer is going to be?"

"Along the lines of 'badass' and 'best thing ever.'"

"You know it."

"Dude, I totally do."

We keep talking until the conversation slowly devolves into pulling out our phones and checking random memes. I sift through my vlog page without thinking and glance at some of the comments when an email pops up. It's from Harper. Immediately, I click it.

from: Harper Knight <PizzaIsMyHeart@gmail.com>

to: Sam Green <TheSamGreen@gmail.com>

subject: OMG

I just saw an ad for a box-set of Stars Wars and Harry Potter mugs. Do you know what this means for my life?????? Awesome things, Sam Green. AWESOME THINGS.

I glance up at Cat, who is busy checking her phone, careful to make sure she doesn't see what I'm doing. Like with my vlog, I'd rather her not know about Harper. I'm not sure why, but I almost feel like I'm somehow cheating on her with Harper. I mean, yeah, it's stupid because Cat is strictly my best friend and Harper is, well... she is the girl I want, but I still feel like it.

That's not a weird feeling to have, right?

I close my eyes. Oh who am I kidding? That's *totally* weird. I have no idea why I feel that way, either.

Finally, I type my response.

from: Sam Green <TheSamGreen@gmail.com>

to: Harper Knight <PizzaIsMyHeart@gmail.com>

subject: RE: OMG

OMG is right. This is groundbreaking! Revolutionary! But when you buy it, promise to a) order a Harry Potter one for me and b) when you get it, put your feet on a table, get a Chewbacca glass, and drink orange soda from it like a boss.

from: Harper Knight <PizzaIsMyHeart@gmail.com>

to: Sam Green <TheSamGreen@gmail.com>

subject: RE: RE: OMG

OF COURSE I'll get you one and OF COURSE I'll drink from the Chewbacca glass like a boss. But it won't be orange soda. I will, being the class girl I am, drink root beer instead.

Because let's be honest here, root beer is a total turn-on.

from: Sam Green <TheSamGreen@gmail.com>

to: Harper Knight <PizzaIsMyHeart@gmail.com>

subject: WHAAAAT

I am now picturing you sitting on a beach chair and getting fanned with giant green leaves by servants on either side of you while you drink your root beer out of a Chewbacca glass (like a boss) and stare at a hot guy by the pool. (The hot guy being me, obviously, with ripped abs and biceps and perfectly tanned skin because that's just how I look.)

Also: is this your screwed-up way of wooing me, Harper Knight?

from: Harper Knight <PizzaIsMyHeart@gmail.com>

to: Sam Green <TheSamGreen@gmail.com>

subject: RE: WHAAAAT

That's exactly how it is. Then you get out of the pool and shake the water off your hair and perfectly chiseled stomach in slow motion with romantic music playing in the background. And after that you approach me equally slowly and we flirt via Chewbacca glass root beer because we are the cliché.

Also: yes, yes it is.

I grin, because Harper just has that effect on me. I'm about to type my response when Cat looks up from her phone and says, "You ready to go?"

"Um." I glance down at the unanswered email. "Yeah," I say, nodding. "I guess. Let's go."

"Cool." She smiles at me, grabs her shopping bags, and we march out of *The Icecreamery*, leaving a tired-looking Sharon and several weirded-out parents in our wake.

Chapter 3

The next morning is a total daze. My alarm goes off too late, and I roll out of bed only to find that school starts in just forty minutes. Just my luck.

I throw on a shirt, race down the stairs, and skid into the kitchen, armed with a glass of orange juice and a bowl of Lucky Charms. It's a Monday, and I am exhausted. Harper and I spent the entire night emailing back and forth to each other, a conversation which started out about school and ended in making fun of celebrities at award shows and lusting for Girl Scout Cookies. I was too smiley while talking to her to sleep or even worry about how shitty I'd feel in the morning, so I guess this whole Curse of the Monday Fatigue thing I'm feeling is my fault. I swear, though, it was so worth it. Talking to Harper is *always* worth it.

Next I pull out a spoon from the drawer by the sink, hop up on the kitchen counter, and speed-eat my breakfast. Milk and cereal go flying everywhere and I'm sure I look like the breakfast equivalent of the Cookie Monster, but I don't care. It's not like the manner standards without Mom here are all that high.

My dad sits at the opposite end of the room. He eats his breakfast of toast and hardboiled eggs without meeting my gaze or so much as acknowledging my presence in the slightest. Dark circles rim his eyes, and even his glasses, which sit atop his thin nose, can't hide the faint bloodshot tone to them. He's been drinking again, I can tell. He's always drinking nowadays.

After a second, a wave of nausea comes over me and I can't look at him anymore, so I try to focus on something else in the room, anything but seeing his face. I shift my gaze to the refrigerator.

It's white and peeling, with photos of Mom scattered all across it. I lean in, squinting a little. Some of them are older, fading pictures of Mom and Dad when they first met as teenagers, of them chasing each other on the beach post-college, and even snippets of their wedding where they're smiling and hugging and looking so happy together—like a real couple. Like they used to be.

Then there are some pictures of me with her, me with dad, me with both of them. A drawing I made of Mom in second grade hangs in the corner of the refrigerator, depicting what's really a stick figure with a straight line over her head that's apparently supposed to symbolize hair, and beside it the note I wrote to her before I left for slumber camp for the first time, as well as a picture I took of Mom wearing shutter-shade glasses about a year ago, after she informed me she was going to become a hipster and "follow the teenage trends." I laughed at her then and made fun of the insane poses she did with those glasses. I mean, she looked like a complete idiot, but she had no shame about it, either. And that's what I miss—how she was her own person, how she never cared what anyone thought, only what *she* thought of herself.

I'm smiling now, but I'm not laughing with her anymore. Just like I have every day for the past six months, instantly, I regret taking her for granted. I regret just assuming she'd be there for me when I wake up in the morning, thinking she'd always be home cooking dinner for me and humming Elvis songs to herself since according to her, "Elvis is a god." I regret not telling her how much she meant to me, how much I'd miss her, how devastated I'd be to see her go. If I could have one more second more with her, I would spend it whispering how much I love her into her ear and hugging her, just hugging her, and not letting go until she's finally slipped away into nothing.

Most of all, I regret losing her. I regret letting her go without a fight, just like that. I don't want to make those mistakes again. I don't want to see anyone else leave, don't want my heart to be ripped to shreds all over again.

I'm almost… afraid to love anyone else again. I want to be happy, and all love has done for me in life is stab me in the back.

After a while Dad looks up from his newspaper and glares at me from the kitchen table. I feel his gaze on me, and I sigh a little, pushing away the memories of Mom. I turn back to him, not wanting to look at him but not having the energy to fight it.

He looks terrible, as usual. Between his fading gray hair, his worn face, and the sad, empty look in his eyes, he looks so bad that I'm almost tempted to pity him. Hell, I *would* pity him, but after treating me and my mom like shit for the past year, the man is going to have to look a hell of lot worse to get any sympathy from me.

"Going to school?" Dad says, scowling.

This time, I don't meet his gaze. I drop my spoon into my half-empty bowl of cereal, suddenly not hungry anymore. "Yes, *Dad*, it's a Monday. That's what normal people do on Mondays: they go to school. Or to work," I add. There is nothing I dislike more than talking to him. Hearing his voice never fails to bring the taste of bile into my mouth, and all of my conversations with him seem to leave me nauseous. I hate my dad, hate how he ignores me, hate what he did to Mom and how he doesn't even seem to care.

"Are you trying to say something about me?" he asks.

"No," I say, hopping off the counter and moving toward the sink, bowl of cereal in hand. The spoon hangs from my mouth. "Of course not."

He glares at me, but I ignore him. "I told you," he says slowly, gritting his teeth. "I can't get a job because I'm busy."

"I can sure see that," I say as I drop the bowl into the sink and turn on the hot water. "That newspaper has been keeping you busy for the last six months."

"It's just so riveting," he spits.

I shake my head and ignore him, not wanting to engage any further. While the water is still running, I kick open the dishwasher and slip my bowl inside. Then I switch off the water, reach into the refrigerator to my left, and grab a ham sandwich lunch I prepared last night. In one single motion, I slip it into my bag and turn toward the door. "Well, I'm off to do something productive with my life. You should consider doing the same," I say, then grab my backpack and walk out the door.

He doesn't respond to that, but I can feel his glare on me as I walk down the front steps, into the driveway, and over to his old car he "lets me use." I'm used to his looks by now, though. It's been like this every morning since Mom's death, so I know the drill.

It's not that my dad's abusive. He's never laid a hand on me, and he most certainly isn't ever going to. He's not that kind of person; he barely even *yells* at me. He's just in the background, a bitter nonfactor in my life. He makes me do it all alone, drinks his beer and makes snide remarks, and never does anything for me—but we *don't* fight. That should be a good thing and maybe it is, but sometimes, I think his complete lack of caring is worse than fighting.

Fighting, at least, means I still matter to him.

Not caring doesn't.

Right before I step into the car, I turn around. Through the foggy kitchen window, I meet his gaze and feel my throat catch. He just looks at me, his eyes hard, his lips curled.

***

I pull into the parking lot of my tiny high school a few minutes later and look around.

The school itself is only two buildings, a main one with two floors that are each divided up by subject and with a miniscule gym sitting behind the first. There is an athletic field surrounding the gym, but it's the only field we have—depending on the season, it serves as the football field, the soccer field, the lacrosse field, and the field to every other sport students play here. The school is old, red-brick, and constantly surrounded by a thick mist, and as I step out of Dad's car and walk up to the front entrance, the dew-covered grass wets my sneakers. The school is isolated atop a steep hill (known simply as "Hill Street"), like a special little sanctuary that achieves my one goal at the moment: to get away from the rest of the world.

Technically my school is a private school, but it costs almost nothing and teaches at just about the same pace as the local public high school. The only difference is this high school is much smaller, only about fifty kids per class, which is why my mom wanted to send me here. It isn't a bad school, though. The kids are nice, even if I don't really connect with them, and the work here is decently-challenging. Plus, the small class sizes and the fact that I rarely ever socialize with the other kids in town who don't go here means no one knows about my vlog series.

A cool breeze brushes past me as I race up the steps to the school entrance. This early in the morning, the smell of moss is everywhere, probably from one of the trees surrounding the school.

It's still too early to function beyond sleep-zombie status, I remind myself as I step inside, yawn, and make my way down to my locker. Cat's is only a few away from mine, decorated on the inside with pictures of chocolate cake and pizza (it's like she's *trying* to kill me.) She nods at me as I approach. The faint scent of her vanilla shampoo fills my nose.

"Monday," she says with fake enthusiasm and gives a small pump of her fist.

I grimace and quirk my eyebrow. "Fun times." Then I turn, empty my backpack into my locker, and pull out my laptop. There are still a few minutes before class, so I lean against the wall, sit down, and scroll over to my vlog page. No new messages from Harper. My heart sinks.

Cat's locker slams above me. "Well, I gotta get to Math," she murmurs, grabs her backpack, and walks in the opposite direction down the hall. "Bye. Talk later?"

"See you," I say without looking up. "And yeah, we'll talk later."

She disappears after that.

A few other kids trickle down the hall after me, grab books from their lockers, and head to class, but instead of following their lead I wait and focus in on my computer. The faint hum of the heater reverberates throughout the hallway, and it's working so hard it smells like something is burning.

Next I check my email, hoping to find something new from Harper in my inbox. Sure enough, I am right. I grin a little as I click on it, already giddy to see what she has to say this time.

That's what Harper does to me, though. She makes me feel

so, so giddy.

from: Harper Knight <PizzaIsMyHeart@gmail.com>

to: Sam Green <TheSamGreen@gmail.com>

subject: your life just got better

So I got bored last night and taught myself how to make a GIF.
So naturally, I made my first GIF to be of a cow. The result is pretttttty
freaking awesome.

Then, she pastes a link. I click it immediately. A new window

opens, and the next thing I know I'm staring at a GIF of a cow

standing on top of a bike doing the disco with its hooves or whatever

it is you call cow feet while also balancing a piece of pizza on its head.

Tumblr fame, Harper writes after the link, *here I come.*

I stifle a laugh. A girl from English spins around and shoots me a condescending, "WTF is wrong with you" stare, then continues fast-walking down the hallway. My face totally flushes. God, I must look like a total idiot, laughing in front of my computer on a Monday morning. I mean, seriously? Who does that? If only the girl knew I was talking to my internet girlfriend. Then she'd really think I was insane.

After another minute of staring at Harper's GIF (to soak it in, of course) I type my response.

from: Sam Green <TheSamGreen@gmail.com>

to: Harper Knight <PizzaIsMyHeart@gmail.com>

subject: RE: your life just got better

That is either the most awesome or the most horrifying thing I've ever seen in my life. I can't decide which.

Harper replies right away.

from: Harper Knight <PizzaIsMyHeart@gmail.com>

to: Sam Green <TheSamGreen@gmail.com>

subject: RE: RE: your life just got better

Both?

from: Sam Green <TheSamGreen@gmail.com>

to: Harper Knight <PizzaIsMyHeart@gmail.com>

subject: DON'T YOU GO TO SCHOOL?!?!

How did you respond so fast?!

...is someone anxious to talk to a certain charming and entirely attractive guy? ;-)

from: Harper Knight <PizzaIsMyHeart@gmail.com>

to: Sam Green <TheSamGreen@gmail.com>

subject: RE: DON'T YOU GO TO SCHOOL?!?!

Three things:

> 1) *Yes, I go to school, and it is terrible, and that is okay.*
>
> 2) *That is such a lie. Get over yourself, Green.*
>
> 3) *There is something utterly terrifying about your use of the winky-face smiley.*

from: Sam Green <TheSamGreen@gmail.com>

to: Harper Knight <PizzaIsMyHeart@gmail.com>

subject: RE: RE: DON'T YOU GO TO SCHOOL?!?!

> 1) *Okay.*

2)   *Please. I'm gorgeous.*

3)   *;-) ;-) ;-) ;-) ;-) ;-) ;-)*

from: Harper Knight <PizzaIsMyHeart@gmail.com>

to: Sam Green <TheSamGreen@gmail.com>

subject: RE: RE: RE: DON'T YOU GO TO SCHOOL?!?!

Those winky-faces are making me shiver. I swear they're going to kill me in the middle of the night and make me into a delicious winky-face stew.

from: Sam Green <TheSamGreen@gmail.com>

to: Harper Knight <PizzaIsMyHeart@gmail.com>

subject: They are.

In their defense, they make one mean smiley face stew.

Especially with added Harper contents.

from: Harper Knight <PizzaIsMyHeart@gmail.com>

to: Sam Green <TheSamGreen@gmail.com>

subject: RE: They are.

You did NOT just imply that I'd make a good stew.

from: Sam Green <TheSamGreen@gmail.com>

to: Harper Knight <PizzaIsMyHeart@gmail.com>

subject: RE: RE: They are.

Oh, but Harper Knight, I totally did.

from: Harper Knight <PizzaIsMyHeart@gmail.com>

to: Sam Green <TheSamGreen@gmail.com>

subject: RE: RE: RE: They are.

Whatever. I am still more awesome than you.

Also, BTW, I wanted to talk to you about something. I'll chat you through our chatroom...

I nod even though she can't see me and glance at the time. My stomach drops. *Oh shit.* I'm a minute late to class already. I type my next email in a complete rush while grabbing my bag and rushing to my first class.

from: Sam Green <TheSamGreen@gmail.com>

to: Harper Knight <PizzaIsMyHeart@gmail.com>

subject: Sry

Actually i gotta go.. ttyl

As soon as I click send, I slam my computer shut, shove it into my backpack, and race down the hall to class, wondering all the way what Harper wanted to talk to me about it.

Chapter 4

from: Sam Green <TheSamGreen@gmail.com>

to: Harper Knight <PizzaIsMyHeart@gmail.com>

subject: Getting wooed

Dear Harper,

Being that I am your gorgeous knight in shining armor, I've decided to woo you with a haiku. So here goes nothing. (Prepare to swoon.)

Chocolate is lovely

Ice cream so wonderful

But you are for me

from: Harper Knight <PizzaIsMyHeart@gmail.com>

to: Sam Green <TheSamGreen@gmail.com>

subject: RE: Getting wooed

Dear Sam,

First of all, the idea of you "wooing" me is laugh-worthy. You are not smooth in that way. Second, that haiku was seriously terrible. No swooning here.

He can't write haikus

He is no good at wooing

But I still like him.

Dear Harper,

Um, you totally did swoon. I'm your knight in shining armor. I am wonderful. And your haiku was somehow even worse than mine.

Forget all the ice cream

Forget the wonderful sweets

You are mine

(I'm going to speak to you in just haikus from now on...)

That haiku was worse

Somehow you so suck at them

Oh my god please stop

from: Sam Green <TheSamGreen@gmail.com>

to: Harper Knight <PizzaIsMyHeart@gmail.com>

subject: RE: RE: RE: RE: Getting wooed

(Continuing the haiku convo theme...)

My haikus bring all

the girls to the yard damn right

they're better than yours

from: Harper Knight <PizzaIsMyHeart@gmail.com>

to: Sam Green <TheSamGreen@gmail.com>

subject: Hopeless

You are so hopeless

I pity your real friends

You fail at wooing

from: Sam Green <TheSamGreen@gmail.com>

to: Harper Knight <PizzaIsMyHeart@gmail.com>

subject: RE: Hopeless

I am wooing you

But you don't even know it

I am that awesome

from: Harper Knight <PizzaIsMyHeart@gmail.com>

to: Sam Green <TheSamGreen@gmail.com>

subject: Hopeless

Okay… this is getting weird, oh knight in shining armor. Can't you just carry me away to safety? (I can barely say that without laughing. You? Carrying ME to safety? HAHAHAHAHAHAHAHA.)

(Wait for it…)

(HAHAHAHAHAHAHAHAHAHAHAHAHAHAHAHAHAHAHAHAHAH AHAHAHAHAHAHAHAHAHAHAHAHAHAHAHAHAHAHAHAHA)

(There. I'm done.)

from: Sam Green <TheSamGreen@gmail.com>

to: Harper Knight <PizzaIsMyHeart@gmail.com>

subject: HAHAHAHA

You laugh now, Harper. But soon you'll be fanning yourself from my utter gorgeousness.

Now, I leave you with one final haiku. (This one is serious.)

Met you through my vlog

I don't even know who you are

But I need you here.

It takes a few minutes for Harper to respond. I sit there, refreshing the page every five seconds, my hands clenching. Was saying that mistake? Was I too serious? Too forthcoming? Oh god, what if I screwed this up? Oh shit oh shit oh shit. I bury my face in my hands until finally, an email from her pops up. I read it with a pit in my stomach.

from: Harper Knight <PizzaIsMyHeart@gmail.com>

to: Sam Green <TheSamGreen@gmail.com>

subject: (no subject)

Then I will come here.

For you.

(I'm serious.)

When I finish reading, I feel energy coursing throughout my body. My head pounds and a smile breaks across my lips. She will come here? Does that mean—?

Before I can finish the thought, a chat box pops up.

Hey, it reads.

I'm sitting in my room, doing nothing but homework, so I push aside my textbooks and respond. Harper is waaaay more important than math.

Hey, I write.

Can I ask something? Like... something kinda serious?

Of course!

It's kind of a response to that last email you sent, and well...

There's a pause, and I just keep staring at the screen, my curiosity growing with every second.

I know this is going to sound weird, but I was thinking... we've known each for a few months now and I really like you. Like, a lot. And since you only live like twenty minutes away from me, would you... maybe want to meet-up sometime?

Okay.

So.

My heart seriously skips a beat. I feel so suddenly full of energy, like I could run around my house, screaming and dancing and muppetflailing like a boss. Instead I just sit there, on the edge of my bed, grinning like an idiot at my computer. I feel the need to scream

"YESSSSSS!!!!!!" at the screen because *of course* I want to meet Harper, *of course* I want to tell her how I really feel. In fact, I've been wanting this since we first met.

Dream. Come. Freaking. True.

Ummmm yes please? I say instead. *When?*

I was thinking soon!

Like... next week?

Would that be cool?

Yeah. Of course. You pick the meeting spot.

This is going to rule. FYI.

Yeah, the poor meeting spot. It's going to blow up from our combined awesomeness/awkwardness.

It totally is. BUT, you must promise to bring us each a Chewbacca glass so we can drink out of it like awkward badasses. Deal?

DEAL.

Guuuuh this will rule. I seriously cannot wait.

Yes!!! Okay, I gotta go, Sam. Bye!

Peace out, Pizza Cow Ninja.

disappears with dramatic sweep of cape

***

The rest of the day goes by pretty fast. I head to school a few minutes later and whiz through my first few classes. After the day is over, Cat and I meet to do homework and eat dinner at a local Chili's. We don't talk much during it, aside from making fun of our Physics teacher's Albert Einstein-esque hair, and I slip in a few more emails with Harper while she's in the bathroom. Harper and I talk a little more about the meeting place when I come home, and we agree to meet on Friday at a nearby coffee shop.

Three days away.

I of course have not told my dad about the meet-up, nor do I plan to. I'd rather risk getting abducted by a potential pedophile who has been pretending to be Harper Knight, sixteen-year-old girl, this whole time than admit to him I have feelings for someone I met over the internet. I don't know exactly how he'd react, but I'm certain it would start with him laughing at me, commenting on the stupidity of falling for someone online who I've never even seen a picture of, and then he'd eventually find every possible way to make snide remarks with it. "Loser son." "Can't get a date." "Only girlfriend is found through the internet." That kind of crap.

The next day, a Wednesday, flies by equally fast. I don't talk to Cat or Harper or my dad much, just go to school, do my homework, film my next vlog, and go to bed. I don't sleep that night, though. Instead, I spend the whole of it imagining Harper and what she looks like—I've nailed her down as brown-haired, lightly tanned, with green eyes and perfect cheekbones. I wonder how our meeting will go and what it'll be like to finally sit down next to her and just talk to her, person to person, me to her. Will she be as funny in real life as she is online? Will I be charmed by her even more in person?

As I lie there in bed, my eyes closed, I imagine what her laugh sounds like in real life, whether her eyes sparkle, whether her mouth is always curled into a smile like I imagine it is. I wonder what she looks like when she's eating pizza, or how she would dress for Halloween, or what she would be like, fitting into my life. For real. And also, a small part of me wonders whether I'll strike up the courage to tell her how I really feel about her—and, if I do, how she'll react.

But beyond all that, a much larger part of me is scared. Not scared about Harper being a fifty-year-old man (okay, well, kind of that too), but scared of what she'll think of me. Scared she'll decide I'm actually a loser dorky kid, scared she'll think I'm stupid or annoying or whatever it may be. Scared she'll leave me and never want to be a part of my life again.

Even more so, I worry she won't feel the same way about me as I feel about her. I mean, of course Harper and I have talked about "us" and what we are and want to become together. We have plenty of times, especially for an internet couple, but neither of us ever mentioned dating or kissing or any kind of attraction. Sure, she's said she liked me before and joked about sexual things between us, but maybe she means "like" as a friend and the jokes as just harmless comments. Maybe I'm totally overplaying this whole thing.

My heart sinks at the thought, and I run my hand through my hair. Shit. I always assumed we mutually, well, *like liked* each other, but now I realize it was only that: an assumption. She never actually said she liked me that way, and I never asked. I just hoped, wanted it so much I made it true in my head.

A groan escapes my lips. Oh shit shit shit. What if I've been overplaying this whole thing? What if she only sees us as friends and this whole meet-up is so she can properly be just that: my friend? What if, if I tell her how I really feel, she doesn't share the feeling? Or worse, what if she runs right out of my life and doesn't ever return?

Oh god. Oh god oh god oh god. I love her, and as screwed up as it sounds, I really do. But I don't want my love to drive her away.

I turn over in my bed and lie flat on my stomach, my gaze climbing up my wall to the poster Mom made me of her and me and Cat and Dad partaking in our annual Ice-Cream-Eating contest a year ago. We're all grinning and laughing and shoving each other in the picture, being totally normal and totally careless. The sun beats down on us as we stand in front of *The Icecreamery*, our faces smeared with vanilla, making the most random poses we can think of. I sigh at the memory. Why can't this whole thing be as easy and as simple as ice cream? Why can't everything just be sweet, with no other strings attached?

It isn't that simple, though. It isn't ice cream. It doesn't make sense, and personally, I'm not sure it's supposed to.

But for the first time since Mom died, I love someone in my life, and it's sure as hell going to take a lot to stop me from chasing her.

***

The next day, after classes are over, Cat asks me to meet her for an early dinner, and I agree without a moment's hesitation. Anything to keep me from freaking out about Harper and the meet-up is more than welcome at this point.

Cat and I meet at a local Italian restaurant, both of us "dressing up" with relevant meatball and pasta T-shirts—we are incredibly classy people—and as soon as we step inside, the hostess leads us to a red leather booth in the very back of the room. The restaurant is small and warm, with dim lights everywhere and some Italian music playing at a dull hum in the background. The air smells like pasta and garlic bread, and I can hear the laughter of a group of fifty-something adults sitting across from us. We sit down, and the seat feels so soft to the touch. A waitress dressed in a black and white shirt comes over a minute later and pours us water, and we thank her as she moves on to the next table.

"So Cat," I say when she leaves. A dim spotlight overhead shines onto Cat's hair, illuminating it a perfect golden red. We've eaten at this restaurant before, too. Italian restaurants are always a big destination when it comes to our hardcore dorkiness, mostly so we can order breadsticks, get out a white chef's hat, and pretend to look Italian and even talk like it to other customers. This usually results in freaked out looks from random strangers, who Cat and I dismiss as just being jealous of our inner Italian badassery.

"So West," Cat says. Her lips are pursed into a small smile as she skims over the menu in her hand. "I haven't heard much from you this week. What's going on in your life?"

I lean back in my seat, flexing the cramp in my hand. "Just fighting crime. Saving the world. Rescuing small puppies from burning buildings. You know. The usual."

She rolls her eyes. "Wow. You're a really extraordinary person, West."

"The truth is, I do it for the children," I say.

She stifles a laugh. "That's amazing. I'm glad I have someone I can count on when my life is in danger."

"Always," I say. "Just let me know when you are in danger. But I should warn you, you may need to leave a message since being an incredibly sexy superhero is a very tedious and time-consuming gig, with the hot girls chasing after me and all, so you never know when I'll be free." I take a sip of my water, suppressing a smile, listening as the music overhead changes from a symphony of some sort to an opera song. "What are you ordering?" I ask after a while.

"Breadsticks," she says immediately.

I raise my eyebrow. "*Just* breadsticks?"

"Of course. You aren't the only badass here, West Ryder. And breadsticks are the greatest invention known to man."

"Even more than chocolate Oreo cake?" I whistle to myself. This is new territory. Cat *loves* chocolate Oreo cake.

"Hmm. Maybe. Either way, you're now officially on-the-hook to get me both for my birthday next month."

"I would expect no less."

"Good."

"Good?"

"*Good*," she reaffirms, nodding.

The waitress returns about a minute later, takes our orders, grabs the menus, and walks over to the next booth. When she's gone, I turn back to Cat. "I feel like we need to use your breadsticks to look Italian again. Did you bring the hats?"

She reaches into her bag and holds up two white chef hats. "Of course. You doubt me?"

I feign a gasp. "*Never!*"

She smiles. "I'm glad. Now all we need is a fake Italian mustache and accent and we'll be golden."

"YES! And then we can stand at the door saying, 'ze pasta es deliciosa' with our fingers cupped together when customers come in."

Cat takes a sip with her water and wipes her lips with her hands. "West," she says, "you're still terrible at this whole 'don't enforce stereotypes!' thing."

I raise my eyebrow. "I'm Italian myself, so I have an excuse. Obviously."

"*Obviously.*"

Our food comes a few minutes later, and we eat in silence for a long while. I listen to the conversation of the people behind us—a long rant about something political that I don't really follow—and eat way too much of my spaghetti and meatballs. In my defense, the food tastes like it was brought directly down to me from the heavens.

After a while, I sense Cat's gaze on me. I look up at her, but she jerks away as soon as our gaze locks like she's been slapped.

"What?" I say.

Her mouth is full of breadstick as she responds, "Nothing."

"It's not nothing," I say, leaning over to her and putting my hand to her forehead to check her temperature. "Why do you look so weird?"

Color creeps across her cheeks, and she pushes my hand away. I stare at her, frowning some more. This is weird. *Really* weird.

"Nothing," she says too sharply. "*No-thing.*"

"Okay," I say. I don't believe her, but I don't press it, either.

We don't talk much after that, just finish eating, get the check, and converse briefly about my nightly vigils as a superhero and all of the hot girls I attract.

After a while, Cat asks me what I'm doing tomorrow—she says she wants me to come over and study—and I'm almost tempted to tell her all about Harper and how I finally get to meet her, but instead I just shrug and say, "I'm busy."

I swear she doesn't believe me.

Chapter 5

School the next day goes by painfully slowly. First Calculus, then Physics, then History—it's like they're *trying* to kill me. I can't concentrate at all during class, either. All I can think about is Harper Harper Harper and how OMG I'M MEETING HER AFTER SCHOOL and AAHHHH YESSS I NEED THIS and that's pretty much it. It's not like this is abnormal, though, because the classes here don't interest me much anyway—well, except for English. I'm the complete, shameless English nerd. My mom used to make fun of me for constantly correcting her grammar and even pulling that "Knock Knock. Who's there? To. To who? Jeez, Mom, don't you know anything? It's to *whom*!" joke on her. I read a bit too, but not as much as I would want. I'm mostly into English so I can criticize people's grammar and "lack of eloquent word choice" whenever possible.

Anyway, worrying about Harper and how our meet-up will go keeps me well occupied throughout the entire day. I don't think I could name one thing we did in any of the classes.

Finally, after what feels like a century, the last class ends. As soon as the teacher dismisses us, I dart out the door, grab my bag, and race down the hall toward the school entrance.

My pulse quickens. *Holy shit.* I finally get to meet Harper.

"Where are you going?" Cat calls after me, but I just wave my hand and say, "A meeting." Technically it isn't a lie, although it isn't much by way of honesty either. But really, I'm not exactly thrilled by the idea of Cat knowing about Harper. I don't know why, I just want to keep it, like with my vlog, separate from her.

As soon as I burst through the front doors of the school, I run down to the parking lot, hop into Dad's car, and drive probably too fast down to the coffee shop. When I pull into the parking lot of the shop a few minutes later, all of my emotion seems to crash down on me at once. I'm really doing this, I realize, gripping the steering wheel too hard. Four months of waiting and I'm finally meeting Harper.

Again, I repeat: holy shit.

Slowly, I get out of the car and cool air blasts me from all around. I straighten up, taking a breath. Then, with my eyes locked on the coffee shop door, I start walking to the girl of my dreams.

My pulse is pounding as I approach, and each step, each crunch of leaves underfoot, makes my ears ring and makes my whole body get tenser and tenser. *I'm going to meet Harper*, I tell myself. *Oh my god oh my god I'm seriously going to meet her.* In that instant everything that could possibly go wrong seems to race my through my head, and my heart keeps on thudding, thudding, thudding. What if she decides I'm too awkward for her? What if she hates me? What if she takes one look at me, laughs, and walks out? What if I screw up my one shot with her like I have everything else in my life?

I shake my head, trying to push away the bad thoughts because this is supposed to be a *happy* time, but they just keep coming back.

Above me, the sky is cloudy, and it looks vaguely like it's going to rain. There are a few picnic tables bordering the pathway leading to the coffee shop, one of which is occupied by an elderly man reading a trashy romance novel. I grimace. There is something utterly terrifying about an old man reading those kinds of books. I half-expect him to turn out to be Harper in pedophilic form.

When I reach the old coffee shop door, I take one final breath, pull open the brass knob, and step inside, my heart pounding furiously, my mind racing with the possibilities, knowing that there is a good chance I'm about to meet Harper.

And… nothing.

I scan the coffee shop with my hands completely clenched, but aside from a bored-looking cashier and a twenty-something couple feeding each other marshmallows and giggling in a totally non-discreet romantic way, the place is empty. My stomach drops a little and I can feel the disappointment creep in already. I mean, I'm five minutes early, but I still hoped... that I could see her now, I guess. See her for real. Hoped I would not have to worry, to wait any longer for her.

I just want to talk to her already, face to face, so I can tell her how I really feel, so I can finally get it out. And yeah, I obviously want her to feel about me as I feel about her, but even if she doesn't, just loving her is gift enough. She could hate me, she could run away and never come back and even though I'd be hurt, even though I'd spend my nights crying and lying awake thinking about her, it will all have been worth it, because I will have loved her.

Sighing, I sit down, my gaze on the front door. She'll be here any minute, I tell myself. It's both a terrifying and exhilarating feeling: that I could look up any second now and lay eyes on the girl I've been falling for all these months. My hands have not stopped trembling, and as I sit there and stare, it's all I can do not to imagine what will happen when I see her. Will everything go in slow motion like in the movies? Will her face light up when she sees me? Will she run at me and jump into my arms, or just awkwardly walk over, nod, and sit down? And what exactly am I going to say to her, anyway? "Oh hey Harper, you've never even met me before in real life but I'm in love with you and will you marry and while we're at it, let's have kids together!" does not sound like the greatest plan. Then of course my back-up plan is, "uh… hi," which also is not very smooth.

I close my eyes. God, what am I even doing here? It's so much easier to talk through the internet than in real life. She'll immediately realize what a freak I am and then I can kiss goodbye to all hope that I'll ever be with her.

Gaaah. Was this a mistake? Did I rush it? *No,* I tell myself. *She suggested meeting up. Not you. Clearly she's interested.* I take yet another breath. Okay. It's okay.

After a while I lean back in my chair, listening to the sounds of the couple to my right, who are now done feeding each other marshmallows and have moved on to whispering into each other's ears and kissing rather passionately for a coffee shop. It's like they're *trying* to taunt me about being here alone. Without Harper.

I shift my gaze to my left, where a cashier snores softly on the counter. The whole place is painfully quiet.

I just want Harper to get here.

The thing is, I've never seen her before and I'm therefore not entirely sure how I'll recognize her, but I have this gut feeling that I'll know who she is the moment I lay eyes on her. I'll know she's my Harper, the one who I can't get out of my head, the one who I don't *want* to get out of my head. The one who, all this time, I've been falling in love with.

I wait.

My eyes stay glued to the door for several more minutes, but there's still no sign of Harper. After a while longer I pull out my phone and start wasting my time on random apps and memes, as well as by constantly refreshing my vlog page for no real reason. Where is

Harper? She didn't strike me as someone to be late to something like this.

Finally, forty minutes after she was supposed to get here, when I'm just about ready to call it quits and leave, she messages me through our chatroom.

Hey Sam,

Sorry I couldn't make it. Something came up. I feel like an asshole, because I still DO want to meet. Can we try again? Tomorrow maybe? Ugh, still so sorry for not being there. I'm an idiot.

My heart sinks a little further as I read it. I close my eyes, the defeat slipping in. I feel like a pouty five year old thinking this, but I want her here *now*.

Yeah sure… I write. *Okay. Tomorrow. Same time/place?*

Yes! I seriously feel terrible for leaving you. I hope you weren't waiting too long. Tomorrow, yes. I'll be there. PROMISE.

With the Chewbacca glasses?

Hell yes with the Chewbacca glasses. How could you doubt me? Also, I think next time we need to wear something so we each stand out to each other... How about I wear a "I <3 Sam Green" shirt?

Yesss! And I'll have on a custom-made "Harper Knight Is Cooler Than Pizza-Eating Cows" shirt.

And by custom-made I assume you mean made with markers from your house?

Of course.

I would expect no less.

They'll be badass marker drawings, obviously.

Wait, really?

waggles brows Really.

Good. I should never have doubted you.

That is true. Now, promise to bring yourself tomorrow, too, k?

Of course. Prepare to be blown away by my drop-dead good
looks.

Oh believe me, I am prepared, m'lady.

Coolness. See you tomorrow!

Bye!

I start at my phone for a while after she logs off, re-reading the conversation again and again. After the third time, the reality sinks in. A smile flickers across my lips.

Tomorrow, I meet Harper Knight. For real this time.

Chapter 6

I spend my night filming another vlog and thinking about Mom. When I get home, aside from commenting once again on my dad's lack of contribution to the family, I run upstairs, slam my bedroom door shut, pull out my camera, and begin filming. I try not to get upset about Harper, but the sadness just pours out of me.

My words come out in a jumbled mess. I sit on my bed and start talking about losing someone you care about, about death and hopelessness and being lost, and the next thing I know I'm staring into the camera, my heart pounding, my eyes fighting back tears, talking about Mom. "I remember when I was in fourth grade and my mom took Cat and me to the local playground," I say. "It was a normal day—the sun was out, there was a nice breeze, and kids all around us were dancing and laughing and playing on the slides and swings. When we got there, Cat and I squealed about how incredibly awesome the whole place looked. Then, she ran to the playground. I turned to Mom before following her, though, not wanting to abandon my mom. When I hesitated, she said to go on, that we had the whole afternoon to play, that she'd be there waiting. So I raced after Cat, grabbed her hand, and we headed first for the sandbox, where we built a replica of cake and then destroyed it, a process that slowly devolved into a sand-fight. Next we ran to the swings, then the slide, and we laughed and played and laughed some more. It was a great day, full of life and more importantly, full of my best friend. But, after a while, I remember turning back to look at Mom. She was watching me, her eyes sparkling and trained on mine, a huge smile on her face. Then I asked her if she was coming too."

I shake my head and grit my teeth. What am I even doing? Filming this? Spilling out all my inner emotions into a freaking *camera*? God, I really am hopeless. Pathetic. Maybe Dad is right; maybe I am a waste of space. I mean, it's been six months. Shouldn't I be past the crying stage? Shouldn't I have moved on by now?

I take another hard breath.

I don't know whether I should be.

I just know that I'm not.

"She just smiled and shook her head like she knew something I didn't. Then, she knelt down in front of me and said, 'I love you, West. Now go on and play with Cat. I'm always going to be with you, watching and smiling from here. And even when I'm not *here* here, I'm still going to be with you. In here,' she said poking at the ribs near my heart. At the time, I had no idea what she was talking about, but I still remembered it, and I think that was her point. It's like she knew she was going to die on me and said that so that now," I say into the camera, "whenever I think about her death, I remember that day, and I realize I'm not so alone after all."

I tap my heart.

Then, my hands shaking, I reach out and turn off the camera.

I don't publish the vlog, though, and I know I never will. It's not something that will ever go on my channel; it's not funny. It's just a video for me.

As stupid as it sounds, sometimes I just need to let out what I'm feeling. I usually ramble like this to Cat, who hugs and comforts me and makes me feel all warm and tingly again, but sometimes it doesn't feel right to tell her. I don't know why, but it just doesn't. Talking to my best friend about love? That's weird, right?

Point is, I don't tell Cat everything. And since my therapist is a freaking idiot and my dad is useless, oh, and my mom is dead, I turn to my camera, the only thing that keeps me sane nowadays. I always feel my best talking into my camera, and I make a lot of vlogs I don't post—they're just there to make me feel confident again, happy and light inside.

I shake my head as I put away my camera. Jeez, I really *am* insane.

Strangely, though, as I finish the vlog and turn to my computer to distract myself with emails from Harper, I feel kind of... good. Relieved, even. Like for the first time in the six months since my mom's death, I feel a little bit of closure.

***

The stars are out as I walk a couple of blocks down the road to Cat's house. The night sky is midnight blue, and there are no clouds shielding the moon. Aside from the distant whistle of a slight breeze through the tree branches and the chirping of crickets all around me, the whole neighborhood is silent. I walk slowly, calmly, letting the cool air brush against my skin, taking in the distant scent of fallen, rain-glazed leaves. A shiver races up my spine, but it's a nice shiver, a calming one. I should be freaking out now, with that video I made and my meeting with Harper tomorrow, but I feel oddly calm, like the night has stripped me of all fear.

When I reach the end of Cat's street, I stop. Her house is three times the size of mine between its new coat of green paint, its three stories of floors, and its—wait for it—*working doors*. It's practically heaven compared to where I live. The grass in Cat's front yard is entirely green, and her family even has a garden that's blooming with roses, marigolds, and flowers I don't even recognize. It's a nice house, warm and safe and comforting. I know it like it's my own home, and maybe, in a way, it is my own; I'm sure I've spent more nights here in the last year than I have in my real bed. Hell, I'm here so much that the Davenports even nicknamed their guest room "West's room."

After a second, I turn my gaze back to the driveway where I lay eyes on Cat. She sits on the edge of her dad's old red Mercedes, her long, slender legs hanging over the hood, her sparkling blue eyes trained on me. She's dressed in ripped-jean short-shorts and an old white T-shirt. Moonlight pours down on her red hair, giving it a silvery glow. I let out a breath. If I weren't her best friend, I'd think she looks really, well… attractive.

I push the thought away as soon as it pops into my head.

"Hey," I say slowly, walking up to her.

"Hey." She cocks her head to the side when she gets a closer look at me. "You okay?" she asks, frowning.

"Wha—" Automatically, I reach for my face, trying to figure out what she's talking about. Then I remember the pink around my eyes—the dried tears.

"Oh. That," I say. I shake my head. "That's... nothing to worry about."

"You sure?"

"Yeah."

She doesn't look convinced, but she doesn't press it, either.

I take a step forward. "You still fixing that up?" I say to change the subject, nodding toward the car.

She gives a distant little half-smile. "Yep," she says, patting the hood.

Cat has been working on that car for three weeks now. When her dad owned it, it used to be a great car, sleek and slim and luxurious, but the years of wear her dad gave it left it in its current state: peeling paint, failed engine, damaged interior, and scratches all over.

Cat drives her family's truck, but her dad always promised her that if she could fix up the old Mercedes, it would be all hers. He loved the car, and so did she—so she took the challenge. Every night since, she's been working on fixing it.

"It's looking nice," I say, which is a total understatement. Apparently, Cat is extremely handy, because the car appears a hell of a lot better than before.

"You think?"

"Yeah. Not long now," I say and sit up on the hood beside her.

She nods but doesn't look at me. "Maybe in a few months."

For a minute, we just stare up at the stars together, with our thighs so close to touching, not meeting each other's gaze. It's perfect out, and the combination of the fresh air and Cat's presence almost makes me forget—about my mom, about my dad, about

Harper. I shift over to get more comfortable, and my side presses against hers. A shock of warm electricity flows through me at the contact, and I feel my muscles tense up. But I don't move away. I just clench my jaw and turn back to the night sky. I get so lost in her warmth and the breathtaking beauty of the stars at night that I almost forget I'm touching her. When I realize what's happening, though, I mutter an "Oh" and jerk away.

She grimaces. "You're really smooth, West," she says and laughs to herself—a distant, sad kind of laugh.

"Correction: I'm wonderful."

"Correction: you're an idiot."

"Correction: you suck at corrections."

She rolls her eyes. Then, as if she's remembering something, she reaches into her pocket and pulls out the small photograph of her grandparent's beach house, a big place in Florida overlooking the ocean, with a beach all to itself. "My grandpa always promised me I could spend a week there whenever I want," Cat says, tracing her thumb along the picture as she holds it out for me. "You know," she continues, and brings her gaze back out to the moon above us, "I keep dreaming that when this car is all fixed up, maybe I can take it there and stay for a week with a company of some boy I like, just us and the beach and the wind and the water and our shared warmth." She says it like she's telling me about a magical promise land, with that distant sparkle in her eyes, that vague smile flickering across her lips. Even in the darkness, I can see she means it.

Then, without thinking or even realizing what I'm doing, I reach out and push her hair to the side so I can see more of her face. The smell of her coconut shampoo wafts into my nose. I breathe it in slowly, savoring it. She turns to me as I do it, the smile still glittering on her lips.

Both of Cat's parents are workaholics who never seem to be home, and since she, like me, is an only child, she has practically raised herself. I remember coming here when we were kids, and even back then she could make me breakfast, lunch, and dinner, could care for me and care for herself and put us both to bed even though her parents wouldn't be back until early the next morning. She's always been the responsible one, the smart one, the one I can count on no matter what because she's just that great.

"Oh?" I say, quirking my eyebrow. "Is there a boy in your life I should know about?" I give her a playful push against her shoulder.

She rolls her eyes. "Just this idiot one, unfortunately."

"Uh-huh. Now *that* I do not believe."

"You don't?"

"I don't."

"Maybe you're right," she breathes.

I shift closer to her. "Cat... you look really weird... what's wrong?"

She just sighs, ignoring me. "What if I told you I had my sights set on one guy in particular?"

"Then I'd ask you who."

She shakes her head, smiling a little. "But let's just say you can't ask me, or I can't tell you, or something like that."

"Oh," I say, and I stare back out at the empty neighborhood before us.

"And what if... what if I was afraid to tell him?"

I frown. "Who are you talking about? If you tell me I can hel—"

"It's a hypothetical," she cuts in. "But just answer the question."

I give her a dubious look. "Well, in my experience, hypotheticals are always real... but I guess I'd tell you to go for it. It's always better to try and fail than to not try at all. And what's the worst that could happen? The guy will turn you down and turn out to be a douche. He'll just be missing out and you'll find someone better. I know you will," I say, meaning it.

"You really think anyone who turns me down is a douche?" she whispers, looking up at me. I'm consciously aware of how close her lips are to my own, and I really don't understand why.

"Of course," I say, then frown again. "...why?"

"No reason. But okay," she says, nods, and goes back to studying the car like she's hiding something on her features. "I think I'll do that," she finally says. "If this weren't a hypothetical, that is."

"Now are you going to tell me who this guy is?" I say.

"It's no one, I told you."

"Yeah, suuure."

She smiles and rolls her eyes at me. "All right, fine. You caught me. The guy I'm secretly crushing on is that doughboy from the Pillsbury commercials! I've always known he's hot stuff!"

"I KNEW IT!" I shout too loudly, and she shoves my arm playfully and we laugh and laugh until the whole night melts away.

Chapter 7

from: Sam Green <TheSamGreen@gmail.com>

to: Harper Knight <PizzaIsMyHeart@gmail.com>

subject: YOU BETTER COME

School is over. Our meet-up is in thirty minutes. The first one better have just been a LOLJKJK moment and this one turns out to be real.

So.

Be there.

Or else.

I type up the email as I sit in my dad's car in our driveway, thirty minutes before I'm even supposed to leave. I'm too excited to wait, though. I write the email jokingly, but really, I'm nervous. I half

expect her not to show again, to stop responding to my email and for

all this whatever-it-is between us to come to an end, just like that.

I don't want that. Hell, I'd rather have *anything* but that.

Harper and Cat are the two constants in my life, the two who I can

depend on and lean and not worry about being weird in front of or

saying stupid things. I can just talk with them, laugh and be myself

and actually, for once, find happiness. It's like with both of them,

we're in our own little worlds, our special bubbles that there is no

way in hell I want to burst. And to lose either of them is like for my

whole world to split apart—like it did when I lost Mom.

I sigh. My therapist, if she knew about Harper, (and if I were

still her client—Dad deemed her "unfit" after a few weeks, but we

both know it was just because he didn't want to spend money on me)

would probably say this whole internet "love" for Harper is just me

reverting back to my childlike state, trying so desperately to fill the

void Mom's death left in my heart with the first positive thing I found,

and that ended up to be Harper. After all, I met her only a month after Mom's death. But the thing is, if she said that, my therapist would be wrong. Sure, that might be how it started, but Harper is no longer just a filler for my screwed-up life; she's mine. She stole a piece of my heart, a piece of *me*, and that sure isn't filler. That's real.

If only I knew when I first started this vlog that two and a half years later, I'd be here, waiting to meet my internet girlfriend for the first time. Another minute passes before my phone finally beeps. I pounce on it and open up Harper's response.

from: Harper Knight <PizzaIsMyHeart@gmail.com>

to: Sam Green <TheSamGreen@gmail.com>

subject: RE: YOU BETTER COME

Hmm. I'll consider coming. I was planning to go on a date with my other internet boyfriend, but maybe I'll stop by your meet-up too… ;-)

from: Sam Green <TheSamGreen@gmail.com>

to: Harper Knight <PizzaIsMyHeart@gmail.com>

subject: RE: RE: YOU BETTER COME

Ha ha. And you say *I* do the winky face smiley poorly.

from: Harper Knight <PizzaIsMyHeart@gmail.com>

to: Sam Green <TheSamGreen@gmail.com>

subject: RE: RE: RE: YOU BETTER COME

OMG BUT YOU DO!!!! It practically burns my eyes out.

from: Sam Green <TheSamGreen@gmail.com>

to: Harper Knight <PizzaIsMyHeart@gmail.com>

subject: Grrr

gasp *ninja stare*

from: Harper Knight <PizzaIsMyHeart@gmail.com>

to: Sam Green <TheSamGreen@gmail.com>

subject: RE: Grr

Ninja stare?! This is what I mean, Sam! You are an emoticon failure. ADMIT IT.

from: Sam Green <TheSamGreen@gmail.com>

to: Harper Knight <PizzaIsMyHeart@gmail.com>

subject: RE: RE: Grrr

I WILL DO NO SUCH THING!

from: Harper Knight <PizzaIsMyHeart@gmail.com>

to: Sam Green <TheSamGreen@gmail.com>

subject: RE: RE: RE: Grr

sings Emoooooticon failuuuuuuure.

from: Sam Green <TheSamGreen@gmail.com>

to: Harper Knight <PizzaIsMyHeart@gmail.com>

subject: *tosses hair*

Hater. You just don't appreciate my mad talent when it comes to emoticon usage.

from: Harper Knight <PizzaIsMyHeart@gmail.com>

to: Sam Green <TheSamGreen@gmail.com>

subject: RE: *tosses hair*

It pains me to even consider the possibility of you being talented at emoticon usage. It's more like you're emoticonally-challenged. (Yes, I just said that. You're welcome.)

from: Sam Green <TheSamGreen@gmail.com>

to: Harper Knight <PizzaIsMyHeart@gmail.com>

subject: RE: RE: *tosses hair*

Wow.

You really just called me emoticonally-challenged.

Who ARE you, Harper Knight?!

from: Harper Knight <PizzaIsMyHeart@gmail.com>

to: Sam Green <TheSamGreen@gmail.com>

subject: RE: RE: RE: *tosses hair*

The incredibly attractive, charming, and perfect-in-every-way-ever girl you met through the internet. That's who.

I don't respond after that, just smile to myself, turn off my phone, and back out of my driveway. The drive back to the same coffee shop as yesterday feels impossibly long.

I arrive there a few minutes later, clamber out of my car, and head to the door. I glance around the store the second I step inside— no Harper in sight. Then I sigh and take a seat at the same chair as last time. But as I wait there, I realize I honestly have no idea what I'm expecting. For Harper not to show? For her to end up to be a serial killer? For her to decide she doesn't like me and what the hell was she thinking wanting to meet with me and for me never to see or hear from her again? For this all to be a mistake? To go to hell?

It's weird, though, that I don't even care what she looks like. I mean, looks aren't something I'm all that oblivious to, but somehow, today, I don't in fact care. I want to meet *Harper*. Not her face, not her body, not her lips (although I would not complain about meeting those. "Knock, knock," I'd say. "Who's there?" she'd say. "Harper's lips." "Harper's lips who?" "Harper's lips feel so right pressed against mine." Then, we'd kiss, and it would be fantastic. I have it all planned out in my head, okay?), but *her*. If she makes me smile in person half as much as she does online, I don't give a crap about what she looks like. I just care that she's here.

With me.

Sometimes I still try to picture her in my head, though. Blue eyes, brown eyes, green? Long hair, short hair, red, blond, burnette? Dark skin? Slender, pudgy? Freckled, rosy-cheeked? All of the combinations I come up with are beautiful in my eyes, because they are all Harper and I already know Harper is just that: beautiful.

I check my phone—1:23. She should be here by now. My stomach clenches. Oh god, what if she *does* leave me? What would I do if she misses today too?

Another wave of fear grips me as I sit at a small, fake-wood table in the corner of the one-room coffee shop. The place is empty except for a few old ladies across from me, who keep giving me weird looks and gossiping amongst themselves, and the same crappy cashier from yesterday, who is asleep at the cash register again. As is, it's not a very romantic spot for a meet-up, made worse by the fact that this place does not even *sell* coffee. It's like they're trying to drive away customers. With the name "Mary's Coffee Shop," they had one job. *One.* And they failed.

I lean back and try to relax in my chair. It doesn't work, though, because my heart is pounding too hard for me to be even remotely calm. I can't stop thinking about Harper, what's going to happen, how I'm going to react to seeing her. Will she show? Or will I sit here, waiting, for hours and hours? And if she does show, how is it going go to go? Will I work up the courage to tell her how I really feel? If I do, will she reject me? Or say yes and we make out passionately? (That would be the preferred option.) Or worse, what if she doesn't react at all?

Then another thought hits me: she said she only lived twenty minutes away, so will I recognize her when I see her? I shake my head at that. I don't know a Harper in real life. Of course I won't recognize her. Still, even as I think it, I have this inexplicable feeling that I already know her.

After a few more minutes of silently freaking out and getting into staring contests with the old ladies, a message from Harper in our chatroom comes in. I let out a breath of relief I didn't even realize I was holding. At least she isn't dead.

on my way, she says. *sorry. was caught in traffic. see you in a minute.*

get ready for epicness, I respond. I'm smiling now, because above all the anxiety I realize this is really happening. I'm really about to meet the girl I've been thinking about, *dreaming* about, for longer than I can even remember.

okay, I'm here. remember to watch for the I <3 Sam Green shirt, Harper replies a minute later.

Of course. Don't doubt my skills.

Oh, I already do...

Now my whole body is on overload, and I can feel my skin tingling with anticipation. Holy crap. This *really* is happening.

Instinctually, I glance down at my own meet-up shirt, which is really just an old white T-shirt with "Harper Knight Is Cooler Than Pizza-Eating Cows" scrawled across it in fading blue sharpie, as I promised.

I take a sip of water, my eyes trained on the door, trying to remain calm. But I can't. I mean, she's here. She's here! OH MY GOD SHE'S HEEEERE! In less than a minute, I remind myself, I'll meet Harper Knight for the first time.

Just like that, there's a sound at the coffee shop door. A jolt of energy rushes through me, and I lean forward, my fists anxiously clenching and unclenching. I take a deep breath, waiting. The door rattles again, and this time it swings open a sliver, then a little more, until it's finally open all the way. I wait, and my heart seems to leap in my throat. A girl steps inside, but as hard as I try, I can't see her face. Still, I wait.

My whole body is on alert now, and all I want is for the anticipation to end, for me to just meet her already. The smell of vanilla coconut permeates through the room, and I recognize the smell, I'm just too distracted to say from where. I can't look away as

Harper turns toward me, slowly, like in all the best cliché chick flicks,

and I see...

I stop.

I see... Cat?

Cat is walking toward me?

My heart sinks. Why is Cat here? And where the hell is

Harper?

"Hey," she says as she approaches, in a shy, embarrassed kind

way I've never heard her speak to me with before. Her face is red and

glossy, and her vanilla scent engulfs me as she nears the table.

Actually, I realize, this is her flirting voice. Weird. Maybe she just

came from an impromptu date or something?

"Hey?" I frown, but she just blushes and sits down across from

me. I have no idea what's going on. Please tell me Cat didn't find out about Harper and is here to talk some sense into me about meeting her.

"Oh," I say, still entirely confused. "I'm actually expecting someone..."

Her blush fades a little, and she looks at me now, her jaw tight. "You don't notice?" she says flatly.

"Notice what...?"

She closes her eyes like she's debating telling me something, takes a deep breath, and whispers. "My shirt."

Painfully slowly, she lifts up the writing for me to see. My heart rate slows, and then races again. *I <3 Sam Green*, it reads in big, loopy letters. The shirt Harper promised she'd have on.

But how could Cat have on Harper's shirt?

Unless...

Oh my god...

"I'm Harper Knight," Cat whispers, her blue eyes locked on mine. She doesn't move, doesn't flinch, just takes a deep breath and says, "I made her up."

As soon as the words leave her mouth, my mind explodes with thoughts. I feel my insides go cold, and my whole stomach tightens. Harper isn't real? I've been falling for a made-up human this whole? Oh god, oh god, oh fucking hell. Somehow, this is even more pathetic than falling for a sixty-year-old creeper.

"So you did this all... why? As a joke?" I stand up, my hands shaking. This *cannot* be real. My one last chance at love, gone in an instant. I had my heart set on Harper, and this is what I get? A slap in the face?

"No—" Cat starts to blurt out, but I cut in again.

"You're my best friend," I whisper, not turning away from her. "I thought I trusted you."

"West, that's not—"

"Not what?" I shake my head and run my hands through my hair. This can't be happening. This *can't* be. I finally thought I'd found someone, someone for me, and it turns out the person I trust most in this world made it all up? Shit shit shit. What is even going on anymore?

She closes her eyes. "Not... how I meant it," she says softly.

"Then how *did* you mean it?" I'm angry now, and I can't help but let the rage slip into my voice.

This time, she stops. She looks at me, hard and sad. I've never seen Cat look at me like that before. "West?" Her hands tighten at her sides, and I can feel the old ladies watching us with excitement, like we're their newest soap opera. The sad thing is, they're probably right. My life in the past year has been just about the equivalent to that of characters in soap operas. "You really want to know?"

In that instant, by the seriousness of Cat's voice, I know I don't, in fact, want to know. But I'm too curious for my own good. "Yes." I taste bile in my mouth as soon as I say it, and the nausea washes over me in a rush. All I want to do is leave, run away and keep screaming and crying until I wake up from this nightmare.

Cat takes one last breath, reaches out, and brushes the tips of her fingers against my arm. Our eyes lock—hard—and we stare at each other for the longest time before Cat finally whispers, her eyes misting with tears, "I didn't make up Harper because I wanted to prank you. I made her up because I love you."

     ***

When your best friend tells you she loves you, you can do one of three things:

    1)   You can tell her you love her too and then make out with her passionately.

    2)   You can run away.

    3)   Or you can just stare at her for what feels like a century without speaking a word like a senseless idiot and only create more awkwardness for everyone.

Guess which reaction is mine? You betcha. #3. I think it's a solid five minutes of me gawking, not knowing how to respond, not knowing what the hell I'm *supposed* to do, before anything happens. Yeah. That awkward.

My heart is hammering now, and I swear my tongue has refused to work because as much as I try to open my mouth and speak, no words will come out. Beads of sweat drip down my neck, and the throbbing in my head pounds harder, harder, harder.

Cat is in love with me.

Oh my god.

"You know what? Forget it," Cat says when I don't react, shaking her head and gathering up her things. "This was stupid. Forget it ever happened."

"Wait, Cat," I say, reaching blindly for her arm, as if I could possibly make this anymore awkward. (Hint: apparently, I can.)

She pushes past my grip. "No, no…" She grabs her bag, turns, and starts to fast-walk to the exit. "I made a mistake. I shouldn't have… I shouldn't have done this to you."

"Cat," I call after her, but she's already rushing to the door, pulling it open, and getting the hell out of here like I should've done long ago. My whole body screams at me to *just do something* and to *fucking fix this already*, but I can't. I can't think. Can't move. "That's not…" I start to blurt out, but she's already gone. "…what I meant," I finish, dropping my voice, even though she can't hear me.

And now I'm standing in the middle of a failure of a coffee shop that doesn't even sell coffee, with the cashier snoring to my right and a group of three old women staring at me like I'm from another planet and the one person I care about most in this world running away from me. Oh, and also, as if this could get any more exciting, the girl of my dreams doesn't exist.

Somehow, this is not how I pictured the meet-up going.

"Well?" one of the old ladies, who is dressed in her oversized sweater and pink scarf, says. "Aren't you going to run after her?" I don't respond. I just stare at her, dumbfounded, like a complete moron. Words still refuse to come. It's like I'm back in fifth goddamn grade and trying to recite my thirty-line poem in front of the whole school; I have a serious case of tongue-brokenness and no idea how to fix it. "You know if you don't run after her you'll lose her, right? Why would you want to lose your girlfriend?"

"She's not..." I say, shaking my head. "She's not my girlfriend."

The old lady raises her eyebrow. "I noticed the look in that girl's eyes the moment she saw you. If that wasn't the love of a girlfriend, I don't know what it is."

I stop. My heart slows. "What look?"

"Bah," she says, turning to her two old-lady cohorts and sharing a smile like they know something I don't. "Young people these days," she says and the other two burst into sluggish, 90+-year-old laughter. The woman turns back at me. "Hun, from that one look of hers, I know you have a girl who loves you more than anything in the world. That's valuable stuff. Don't let her go."

"Are you... are you sure?" I can't think clearly anymore.

"I am most certainly sure," she says, reaching out a bony hand.

And I must be crazy because now I'm taking advice from random old ladies, but the next thing I know, I run after Cat. I burst through the coffee shop door, cheered on by the three of them, sprint down the sidewalk, and follow Cat's bobbing head over the crowd of people.

I push past stranger after stranger, keeping my gaze trained on Cat, and I just keep running and running. The wind whips against me and the air tastes like cigarettes, but I barely notice any of it. All of my concentration is on Cat now.

When I finally catch up to her, she's fast-walking through another crowd of people, speeding up with each step. I grab her arm and pull her back, breathing heavily. "Hey," I say. She tries to fight my grip. "*Hey.*"

"Let go of me!" she shouts, jerking away from me and nearly taking out a little girl to her right. "I told you I'm sorry! What more do you want from me? Do you want my dignity too? My happiness? My life? Because I'm sure that's just about up for sale at this point." She spins back around to face me, her eyes wild and sad at the same time. Tears sting her eyes, and it hurts to see her like this—like, physically hurts. She looks at me, exasperated. Cat, the strong one who always kept *me* in balance, exasperated. Oh my god, what have I done? "Well?" she says when I don't respond. My jaw is still totally slack. "Aren't you going to say something? I just told you I love you and you have zero fucking reaction?"

I'm consciously aware of my hand on her arm, my skin touching her skin. She is warm and shaking, rattled in a way I've never seen her before. I have no idea what to say, what to do. I feel so fucking pathetic all of a sudden, because she just told me probably the biggest thing you can tell someone and I can't even find the words to respond.

"You really made that account because you love me?" I finally say like a blundering idiot, too scared to meet her gaze, to focus on anything but the slight tremble in my toes.

"I did," she says slowly, watching me as if I'm about to pull I knife on her. I nod. She sighs then, and I watch as she turns her head to look out at the sun beyond the crowded street of people.

"What, Cat?" I ask.

She shakes her head.

I step forward. "Cat," I say. "Tell me."

She hesitates, but does. "Remember when we were thirteen and we decided to prank our English teacher?" she says softly, still looking out at the sun—at anything but my face. "So we snuck into his classroom while he was stuffing his face with chocolate cake or whatever in the teacher's lounge, and we super-glued his markers together? We felt so cool and untouchable at the time, like we'd just reached the holy grail of pranks, and when he yelled at about it to the class the next day just because he wanted to yell, we were giggling like idiots in the back, thinking we were the baddest kids this school has ever seen." She says it with such fondness, with that same twinkle in her eyes from last night, like she's telling me a story of a magical world we'll never quite reach.

I force a laugh. "That teacher was an asshole," I say.

Cat smiles. "Oh god, he so was. Remember his oversized moustache? Man, did that dude need to shave…" She pauses, gathering herself. "Or do you remember our freshman year, when that jerk-y kid Brian beat you out as the JV basketball point guard, and so we spent the whole night plotting how we would commit the perfect murder so you could get on the team like you deserved, and we laughed and laughed until it was morning and time for school again?"

"Or," she says even more quietly, and steps toward me, her body just inches from mine, "do you remember last year, when we visited France because your mom wanted us 'to have some fun for once,' and we sat on that bench in the middle of night, looking out at the city lights and hearing the sound of laughter bubbling all around us, and you touched my arm and joked to me how romantic this would be if we weren't best friends? Do you remember that?"

"Yes," I say. "Of course." And I *do* remember. I remember all of it and more. I think about those memories, about Cat, every second of every day.

She nods and drops her chin so it's hovering just inches from mine. "Those," Cat says, "were the moments I realized I was in love with you. I mean, I thought it was just a weird screwed-up platonic love at first, because I'm not the kind of person who is pathetic enough to fall for her own best friend, I'm just *not*, but the more I thought about it, about us, about *you*, I knew I loved you. Like, for real. And call me crazy but for once in my life, I didn't have any doubts." She looks up. Meets my gaze. I can't turn away. My heart rate keeps slowing and then speeding up again and I don't even know what to do. My whole face feels sweaty, my body a bundle of anxiety. "I knew I loved you," Cat continues. "I knew with 100% certainty that you were the one for me. You know how I haven't been dating for the past year? It's not because I was too busy, like I told you. It's because I was already in love with one boy." She steps closer. Her side touches mine, and I'm flooded with her warmth as well as a sharp, tingling sensation down my spine. "And, West Ryder," she whispers, "that boy was you. But I knew I couldn't just tell you. Or maybe I could, maybe I *should have*, but I was too confused and desperate to do anything but hide it and pretend it never happened, and that it wasn't real, because maybe I just had a bad day and was going crazy." She sighs. "I knew about your vlog," Cat says quietly. "I've known about it forever. You're my best friend, West, and you're an idiot for thinking you could keep it from me." She forces a smile.

I stand there, my mouth hanging open, still trying to process everything she's saying. Finally, I manage to say, "How'd you find out? About the vlog, I mean."

"Dude. You left your diary wide open, flipped to the page with all your vlog info. I saw it when I beat you home from school. You aren't the best with keeping secrets, especially not from me. Hell, *no one* can keep secrets from me."

I blush, and she continues, the distant smile on her lips already fading. "And so there I was with love I didn't know what to do with and a vlog I wasn't supposed to know about. I was desperate, and I decided to combine the two, and I used your vlog to do it. I created a fake profile and started commenting. I didn't know what I was doing—I was being stupid, that's what I was doing—but I just thought… if maybe I could befriend you there, you would see how perfect we are together, without the confusion and weirdness of us also being best friends. And on top of that, you would see how I really do love you… and maybe, just maybe, you could love me back."

There's a long pause before Cat continues. I don't say a word, still dumbfounded like a fucking moron.

"I know everything about you, West, and you know everything about me. We've never had to hide anything from each other. But that day, and every day after that, I had to hide something from you, something most people would tell the whole goddamn world about." She takes a deep breath, and our eyes lock. "I had to hide my love for you," she whispers. "And that first meet-up, I or Harper or whoever the hell you want to call me, didn't miss it because I was caught in traffic. I missed it because I was scared. Scared," she says, "of this. Scared of *you*."

Then, she stops, and takes a step back. My head throbs, and I feel my blood getting hotter and hotter. Cat loves me. My best friend *loves* me. How am I supposed to feel? Shocked? Happy? Scared? I sure as hell feel none of those things, mostly just straight-up confusion, although my heart won't stop beating and my mouth refuses to work properly. And, in the back of my mind I wonder: do I love her back?

But I don't know.

I just don't know.

"What do you want me to say?" I look up at her, and she looks back at me. She's tall, almost as tall as I am, her long red hair a major contrast to my dirty blond. I used to joke with her about how her head was like a red velvet cupcake, with that red-velvet-looking hair and pale skin and perfect smile to go along with it.

I love that smile.

It's just a line now, though—a twisted, sad line.

Her eyes level with mine. Her breathing is even and sounds somewhat pained as she whispers, "I want you to tell me if you'll give this a shot."

"Give what a shot?" I ask, but I already know the answer.

"If you'll go on one date with me," she says, "like we've never met before, and just… see. Just try to be together—as a real couple."

I look at her, but I don't speak. I realize then that it would be so easy to say yes, to tell her I'd love to try this, to tell her what the hell and go for it because I can, because I don't want to see her go

and because what if I do love her and don't know it? But somehow, I

can't find the courage to say it.

I still feel so sick, so empty and tired, and I have no idea if I'll

ever be able to process all this. I have no idea how to respond to her,

either.

"West, please just answer me," Cat whispers. "I've waited

years for you. Just give me a response."

I take a deep breath, my jaw clenching. What am I supposed

to say? Yes? No? Maybe? I'll think about it and get back to you? All of

the answers feel wrong, somehow, and I realize there is no way out of

this but the truth.

"No," I finally say, turning away from her. "I'm sorry, but no."

All at once, Cat's smile slips, and she shakes her head a little.

"Thought so," she says quietly, in a way that's so serious and empty

at the same time that I feel like I've done something horribly, horribly wrong. Then, she turns, brushes past me, and walks down the street until she disappears out of sight.

I almost don't see the tears in her eyes.

***

Everybody seems to be watching me as I walk home. I keep my head down, not meeting their gazes, but I still see their eyes. All of them are strangers, dressed in business clothes or coats or whatever as they rush down the sidewalk to get out of work, but they all seem to be giving me the same disappointed look. It's like they know what I did. It's like they know I broke my best friend's heart. I feel like they're taunting me, guilting me, because these strangers, stares and all, must know what a hopeless idiot I am to turn away the one person I have left in the world.

I take a deep breath. Each step I take seems to fall in rhythm with my pounding heart—*step, beat, step, beat.* The air is thick all around me, and I feel my mind slowly fade out. All I hear is the sound of my heart and each of my footfalls, and the background noise seems to disappear. I keep fast-walking until I reach my car, step inside, slam the door shut, and back out of the parking lot.

The only thing I can think about on the drive back is Cat. Cat Cat Cat. I want to cry, want to scream and pound the steering wheel until this all goes away, until Harper ends up to be real and Cat and I can stay best friends and not... not this. Anything but this.

Cat is in love with me and I turned her down.

Oh shit. That really happened, didn't it? I really turned her down. And she walked away like I'd just punched her in the face. Shit shit shit. I feel like I made a mistake somehow, like I should've done something more to fix this. I mean, she's my *best friend*. Why couldn't I have just manned up and given it a shot? What am I so scared of? I loved Harper, and if Cat is really Harper... what's the difference?

I turn out of Main Street and make my way to the back roads toward my house, kicking myself internally over and over again. But I can't love Cat, right? We're friends, best friends, but we aren't the kind to date. We wouldn't date. We *can't* date.

I've only ever truly cared for four people in the world: my mom, my dad, Cat, and Harper. Now two of them are gone and one is just about gone to me. Cat is the only person left. I grip the steering wheel harder. I'm not letting her go. I'm not going to fall for her—like, for real—and only have my heart ripped to shreds again. I care about her and I love her like a friend, but that's all: like a friend.

I turn another corner. My head is throbbing again. I feel like I should've known Cat was Harper, or at least guessed it. I should've prepared myself for this, thought about it, given her a real response. But Cat being Harper makes so much sense. They both talk alike, think alike, and they both make me feel warm and happy inside. I only mesh with one person in the world as much as I mesh with Harper, and that person is Cat.

Because Harper isn't real, idiot.

I still remember the night Mom died. I was sitting in my room, filming for my vlog, when it happened. Dad and Mom went out for a date night an hour earlier. They'd been fighting so much lately that they said they needed to "reconnect" for a while, which so clearly would not happen, especially because they had a heated, hour-long debate on where to even go to dinner beforehand. They ended up compromising on some cheesy French restaurant, which served alcohol for my dad and wasn't filled with screaming sports fans for my mom. I knew the night would end in them fighting some more, of course, so I distracted myself with my vlog, hoping it would all just go away and we could be a family again—a *real* family.

What I didn't count on was for Dad to get drunk or wasted or whatever the hell he was.

What I didn't count on was for him to get so worked up that he forced Mom to let him drive because "that bitch would try to kill him" if she were behind the steering wheel.

What I didn't count on was for him to run a red light to "get home faster" and for a truck at their right to crash into the passenger door.

What I didn't count on was for my mom to die.

When I got the news, it was late into the night—really late. Even after factoring in the time for them to scream at each other by the car after they stormed out of the restaurant (this happened a lot), I knew it was still taking too long. The air felt off, and when the doorbell rang midway through my filming, I could tell immediately that something was wrong. I knew it like you know how someone is watching you, or how you know the book you're about to read is going to be the best thing ever. I knew it—*I knew it*—and I did nothing.

It was the policeman who told me the news. He showed up at my door, his eyes so empty of life, and he said my dad was arrested and my mom... well, my mom was dead.

At first, I didn't know what to do. I just stood there, shaking, wanting to scream and cry until this all went away, but I couldn't find the energy to do any of it. So then I did nothing. I didn't cry, didn't beg him to tell me he was lying, that this wasn't real, that my mom wasn't really dead. I just looked at him, my jaw set, nodded, said thank you, and shut the door. As soon as he left, though, I fell apart. I cried and cried and cried. The tears quickly turned to rage, then rage to exhaustion, then exhaustion back to tears.

I called Cat soon after. It was the middle of the night and she had a big exam the next morning, but she still rushed over and spent the whole night comforting me, holding me close and telling me it was all going to be okay, that she was here for me and it was going to suck big time, but we would make it through—together. At the time, I didn't believe her. Hell, I yelled at her more times that night than I have any other. But she was right. She gave me a shoulder to lean on. She made everything so much more bearable and asked for nothing in return.

I shake my head as I turn down my street. It's sunny out, cloudless and cool and the perfect autumn day. I pull into my driveway, hop out of Dad's silver Chevy, and walk up the front steps.

Cat was always there for me. Strong when I wasn't. Positive when I felt hopeless. And the one time she needed me, I turned her down.

I never even gave her a chance.

Chapter 8

The next day is Saturday, and I spend it eating ice cream, filming another vlog, and going over my conversation with Cat in my head again and again. I get nothing from it, though.

I don't sleep at all that night or the next, and soon Saturday drags into Sunday which brings me right back to Monday. Before I know it I'm standing outside my high school, hoping like hell I won't run into Cat, at least not yet. Even after two whole days of preparation, I still don't know what to say to her.

As soon as I burst through the front entrance of the school I fast-walk over to my locker, keeping my head down, not meeting anyone's gaze. Cat and I are not exactly the most sociable people so it's not like she told any of *them* about what's going on, but still, like with the strangers on the sidewalk, I can't meet anyone's gaze without getting that sinking feeling that they know what I did.

I glance around the hallway as I pull open my locker, checking to make sure no one is coming. When there's no Cat in sight, I let out a deep breath. *Thank god.*

After another minute I've shoved all of my binders into my locker, grabbed my books, and have started to hurry to class. I still haven't talked to Cat since Friday, but I really don't know what to say. She just seemed so upset at the time that I'm... well, I'm afraid. Afraid that I might hurt her more than I already have. Afraid that I might ruin our friendship.

Well, at least I have more time to worry about it, I say to myself as I slam my locker shut and start down the hallway. But the second I turn around, I run into Cat, who also seems to be trying to slip past me. My book connects with her arm, and her backpack with my face.

So we stand there, eyes on each other, Cat looking angry and me entirely terrified.

Yep. Just our luck.

"Oh, sorry…" I mumble, staggering back. Once I've regained my balance I try to move past her again, hoping like hell to avoid conversation.

"Yeah," is all Cat says. In that instant, I have an overpowering urge to keep on walking, to hurry up and get the hell out of here, but as I look at her, at the sadness in her eyes, I know I can't leave her. I feel so wicked for not wanting to talk to her, but really what am I going to say? "Hey I'm sorry I rejected you but I guess I don't love you like you love me. Screw that, though, let's just stay best friends, kthxbye" would not play in my favor, and that's the best I can come up with.

The thing is, though, it's as simple as that: we *are* best friends. And she is hurt. I'm not going to leave her when she needs me. Sure, maybe we aren't made for romance, but that doesn't mean we need to turn this into something more than it is.

"You okay?" I finally say, withholding a sigh. This was a mistake. This was *so* a mistake.

"Oh, fine," she says. "I've just pissed off my best friend and also made a fool of myself in front of him. So yeah, I'm *splendid*."

I shake my head. Other students file by us, and the whole hallway is a blur of laughs, shouts and smiling faces. That is, except for Cat and me. I move toward her, dropping my backpack against my locker. "Cat, I'm sorry," I say, because I can't think of anything better. "I was an idiot before."

"You don't say?" Seeing her this wound up and knowing it's all because of me sends a jolt of pain rushing through my body. Problem is, I don't know what to do. I don't know how to fix this. Tell her I'm sorry? That sure didn't work. Give loving her a chance? But doing that would go against every fiber of my being.

"Cat, please. What do you want me to do? I really am sorry and you didn't embarrass yourself. It's my fault. I just… I'm just…"

"You're just what?" Her hands are on her hips now, and it looks like she's ready to walk out on me for good.

"I'm just confused," I say, exasperated. "I don't know what to do, Cat. I'm lost. You caught me by surprise, is all."

"Well I'm *sorry* I 'caught you by surprise' and made you feel so lost. That was really selfish of me, wasn't it?"

"You know that's not how I meant it."

"And you know I don't care! Now if you'll excuse me, I have to get to class. We can talk more about this some other time."

At that, she whirls around and starts walking in the opposite direction down the hall. More students rush in, and I can smell her vanilla shampoo unmistakably against the masses of people. "Cat..." I grab for her arm, but she shakes off my grip, giving me a disgusted look.

"Nope. I'm buuuusy, West."

"Cat, c'mon, *please.*"

"Please what?" she says sharply, spinning back around to face me. Her eyes are wild, and her red hair flies everywhere. "Please stop loving you? Please ignore my feelings and let you have you want *again*? Please pretend none of this ever happened? Because guess what, West, it did. And this is one thing you're going to have to face on your own."

"Cat!" I say. "I'm not asking you to stop loving me. I'm not asking you for anything. I just want us… to be normal," I finally say.

She backs away, laughing to herself. "You really think it's that simple, West?" she says, shaking her head. "You think I can just put away my feelings for you, lock them in a box, and ignore them until you're 'ready for them?'"

"No, that's not what I meant—" I start to say, but she isn't listening.

She steps an inch closer. "Just ask yourself this, West," Cat says, dropping her voice to a hushed whisper. "Will you ever be able to stop loving your mom? Because it's the same thing with you and me."

Before I can react, she turns back around, and for an instant all I see is her red velvet hair and the flash of deadly serious blue in her eyes.

"Cat, wait," I choke out. "Please, just wait." But she's already pushing past me, rushing down the hallway, until she turns the corner and disappears out of sight.

I'm left standing there in the middle of the hallway, holding my overly-heavy backpack and wondering if we can ever go back to being normal again.

***

I don't see Cat for the rest of the day, which I'm pretty sure is to both of our benefits. Another conversation with her would be... I don't know. Bad. Just bad.

As soon as school ends, for once, I don't wait for Cat to get out of class so I can walk home with her. I run the distance all myself, not once slowing. When I'm home, I trip up the staircase and stumble into my bedroom. I slam the door shut behind me, sit down on the edge of my bed, and bury my face in my hands.

Oh shit oh shit oh shit. What have I done? I want to cry again. In fact, I can feel the tears glistening in my eyes, but I don't let them fall. I *can't* let them fall. Not now. Not anymore.

Sure, Cat and I have fought before. Actually, we've fought a lot. Whether it be which color M&M is the best (blue, obviously), if one of us cheated at a game of FIFA, or even whether I should go out with Renne or Jessica (long story), screaming is not a rarity between us. But this fight… this one was different. It was too sad and desperate. It felt more like the end of something than a true fight, and I just hope this "something" is not our friendship.

God, I really screwed this whole thing up. I just want to punch something, or break down the wall, or whatever it is that will make me feel better and a hell of a lot less alone. Of course it had to turn out this way. Of course the instant I start to feel vaguely happy again after Mom's death, things go to hell. I run my hands through my hair and kick myself in the ankle. Why can't Harper just be real and Cat not love me and Mom come back to life and me and Cat to go back to how things were before? Why does this shit have to keep happening to me? I'd even give up my vlog for Cat. Hell, I'd give up *anything* for us to be back to normal again.

To me, Cat is the sister I never had. We know everything about each other; we mesh like fire and wood. So how did we screw this up? Because of love? *Love?* Aren't we supposed to embrace love? People spend their whole lives searching for it and never finding it, so why is it that the instant I get a little taste of it, it screws me over? Isn't it supposed to be a gift, not a curse? Not something that hurts this damn much?

The worst part is that I don't know if I love Cat. I need her like I need a place to live, like I need a way to express myself. I can be myself around Cat, no judgment, and she can do the same for me. I've never smiled more than when I'm with her, and even when she was Harper, I still couldn't stop smiling. Is that what love is? What Cat and I have? I have no freaking idea how to tell.

Then another thought hits me: how come I was so sure I was in love with Harper before I knew she was actually Cat, and now that I know she was my best friend all along, I'm suddenly not sure? She's still the same person, right? So does that mean…?

I cut off the thought before I can let myself finish. It isn't like that, and I know it.

I let myself slip back in bed. The truth is, I'm scared. I don't know if I love her, but I also don't *want* to love her, because loving her will mean losing her. And losing Cat… well, without her, I'd have nothing, *be* nothing.

"West!" my zombie of a dad growls from downstairs, interrupting my thoughts. "Dinner is ready! Hurry up." Translation: "I'm hungry so go make me some fucking macaroni and cheese while I sit and read this newspaper for the millionth time. I've had a tough day of doing nothing."

I sigh, close my eyes, and stumble down the stairs. I walk into our old, falling-apart kitchen, and I'm sure the dark circles around my eyes are entirely evident. Sure enough, my dad sits at our tiny kitchen table, his feet on the counter, a beer in his hand, and no dinner ready.

"Make me something good," he says and takes a drink. I can smell his disgusting scent, some mixture of alcohol and pure evil, from here.

"Of course I will," I mutter under my breath, "because what else would a son be for other than to serve as his father's slave?"

"You should be nice to me, you know," he says, not looking at me. "My money is the only reason you're alive."

"Your money?" I laugh to myself as I walk over to the cabinet and pull out a pre-made macaroni and cheese. I pour into two paper bowls, one for me and one for him. "You mean your mom's money?"

He doesn't respond to that, and a glimmer of satisfaction races through me. Right now, I'm really too tired to even pretend to be polite with Dad.

It isn't a lie, however. The only reason we still have a house is because of my night job at Starbucks, and also because my dad has convinced his loaded mother to send us money every month to keep us afloat in these "tough times" after Mom's death. In reality, Dad doesn't even seem to care about her death; he just wants his mom's money. All he does is drink and sleep and ignore me. I'm not afraid of him or anything, but I just wish... that he could be normal. That he could not be so fucking useless. That he could treat me like a *real* son and that he could be a *real* father. That maybe, just maybe, he could've been there for me after Mom's death.

But he wasn't.

He never even mentioned Mom's name, or anything to comfort me, before or after the funeral. Not an "it's going to be okay," not a "this sucks," not an "I'm sorry." He never brought it up, so neither did I. When I'm with him, it's like it never happened, like I never even had a mother.

He's claimed to interview for several newspaper gigs since her death, but I know he threw all the interviews on purpose. As long as his mom sends in money every month and as long as I do all the housework for him, he couldn't care less about getting a job.

My dad wasn't always like this, though. He used to be an okay dad, with a well-paying lawyer job and a smile that never left his face.

I haven't seen that smile in so long.

I miss it, honestly.

But all of a sudden, about a year ago, he just gave up. He stopped caring. He quit his job, took to smoking and drinking and enslaving his family members. Things got hard for Mom, for me, for all of us, and my dad acted like he was the fucking king of the world. Mom should have left him then, and we all knew it, but her job didn't pay well enough to support both her and me and we needed his money. Plus, both of us sort of secretly clung to the hope that Dad would get better again and we could go back to being normal, to being happy. To being *a family*.

I don't really know why Dad stopped caring as dramatically as he did. I think it started off as depression from his and Mom's marriage troubles, and then it just spread from there. Dad never said anything, never acted like he was any different than he used to be, and I didn't have the courage to ask. So it was just that: a mystery.

I give him an annoyed look as I pour the water into the macaroni noodles, add cheese from the packet, and microwave both bowls. Dad doesn't look at me; he never looks at me. It's like the sight of his own son is too much "work" for him to undergo, and so he ignores my existence altogether. When the microwave beeps, I pull out the bowls, shove one toward him without meeting his gaze, and then bring my bowl to the corner of the kitchen as far away from him as I can possibly get. On today of all days, I am not getting into it with him.

We eat in peace for a few more minutes, neither of us saying a word—thank god—until Dad finally throws his spoon against the bowl and jerks back in his chair. "This sucks," he says and slams the bowl against the table.

I roll my eyes. "That's interesting, because you seemed to enjoy the exact same thing *just fine* last time."

"I was being nice," he says, tossing his newspaper aside. Finally, I look at him. Dad is tall, unshaven and thick-jawed, with a hard face, dark brown eyes, and a thin smile. He looks sad and rugged, his once jet black hair now thick and gray. In a way, I kind of feel bad for the man. He's clearly lost, and whether or not that's because of Mom's death or his own stupidity, I have no idea and nor do I care.

"Wow, so generous of you," I mutter. "If that's the case, then maybe you can try being a normal grown-up for once in your life and—I don't know—make your own dinner."

"Are you calling me lazy?" he says, sipping his coffee cup which we both know is just hiding more beer.

"No, I'm just calling you useless. There's a difference." I take another bite of my macaroni, sighing to myself. I don't like that this is what Dad and I have become, this empty, lifeless trading of insults, but what else is there? It's better than screaming, right?

Even screaming, though, means we care. It means we're fighting to find a way to be father and son again, for real. But this? This is like we've both given up, and I guess, in a way, I have.

"You're a complete waste," he mutters.

"Of what? Your precious free time?" I push my bowl to the side and hop off the counter. I'm suddenly not hungry anymore.

I can feel his gaze on me, dark and calculating. "You better shut the hell up and show me some respect, West. After all, *I'm your father.*"

I laugh lightly and walk toward the door. "Yeah. My father and respect aren't words that seem to go well together."

"They work fine for me. Much better than 'my son,' at least," Dad says without looking at me. I can see his fists, though; they're curled around his coffee cup. Tightly. It looks like he's trying to squeeze the ceramic until it breaks.

I shake my head, wanting to punch him in the face right then and there but holding the feeling down instead. "Good to talk to you too," I mutter, hop off the counter, and walk into the family room. I sit down, slamming the door shut behind me, with a bad taste in my mouth and a sick feeling in my stomach. The family room is a small room adjacent to the kitchen, complete with fading gray walls, a small sofa, and a TV sitting in the center. We used to spend so much time here, my mom and I, but now it appears to be more of a storage room than anything else, with bin after bin of random supplies stacked all around it.

As soon as I sit down, I turn on the TV to some random station, but I don't pay attention. I just stare blankly at the screen, my eyes glazing over. Fuck. This is really what I'm reduced to. Running and hiding from everyone I know, and retreating to… what? The TV? To my own misery? I have no one now—not my dad, not my mom, not even Cat—and it's all my fault: because I'm an idiot, because I keep telling myself that if I try to love anything else ever again, they're just going to end up like Mom—dead, along with my heart. I can't take that anymore.

For a minute, I just sit there and I think about Cat, who is probably off and making new friends and totally forgetting about me. I can't push her away, not over something this stupid. I can't screw up my life any more than I have.

Then, it hits me. I need to fix this.

Before I know what I'm doing, I reach for my computer, click over to my email, and begin typing. I click send without reading it over, and proceed to constantly refresh my inbox until I get a response, afraid I won't even get one.

from: West Ryder <WestRyderIsPerfect@gmail.com>

to: Cat Davenport <IAmCatWoman@gmail.com>

subject: (no subject)

Dear Your Highness of All Things Chocolate,

It has come to my attention that your subject, West Ryder, has been temporarily banished from your chocolate kingdom due to his "asshole behavior." I've recently been in contact with said criminal, and it seems he can't stop thinking about how stupid he acted and now all he wants is to get you back. So he wishes for me to deliver you this real apology. He says that even if you don't accept, Your Highness of All Things Chocolate, he wants to thank you... for everything you've done for him. Anyway, here it is:

Dear Your Highness of All Things Chocolate,

I am sorry for insulting your chocolate-centric palace and for leaving you so abruptly. I am sorry we fought over which chocolate is best—obviously dark chocolate—and I'm sorry it's come to this. But more than that, I'm sorry for disappointing you. You needed me, and I... I wasn't there for you. I regret it. I want to come back to your Chocolate Palace, but more than that, I want you, Your Highness. I want to be with you again. I want to be your friend. I don't want to push you away any further.

I want to fix this.

With lots of chocolate,

West

(Seriously, Cat. I need you. I don't care what anyone thinks. I need you.)

When I read over the email, I know deep down that I mean every word of it.

It feels like the longest time before Cat responds, but in reality I don't think it's much more than thirty minutes. I keep refreshing my inbox, though, my pulse pounding, wondering what Cat will think. Will she ignore me? Will she even respond?

Finally, my email dings, and I swear it's the most beautiful sound in the world. I rush to click on it, and I take a deep breath. My stomach is tight as I start reading the email, and I swear I'm *expecting* to be disappointed, to be turned down and pushed away for good.

from: Cat Davenport <IAmCatWoman@gmail.com>

to: West Ryder <WestRyderIsPerfect@gmail.com>

subject: (no subject)

Dear Servant,

First of all, it was my direct order for you never to email me again. For this offense, you shall be beheaded tomorrow at dawn. Be there, or we'll just behead you elsewhere. I can wait. I have plenty of chocolate in this palace to last me.

Second, however, I am glad you sent me this email from that West Ryder character. (Though yes, you're still going to die. You are incredibly needy. You say you "must have food and water every few days or else you'll die?" Seems very rather greedy of you.) I

remember him quite well; we used to be close, and I hope we still are,

but we just... disagreed about something, and that was all. I banished

him from my Chocolate Palace because I was angry in the moment,

but I do hope he can return to the Palace soon. Point being, tell him

this before you die:

> *West,*

> *I need you too.*

> *Without pity,*

> *Your Highness of All Things Chocolate*

By the end of the email my heart is in my throat and my whole body feels so light inside. I let out a breath of relief.

I need you too.

They're just four words, but they've already sent my body into an episode of muppetflails, internal screaming, and excited jumping-and-down. The knot in my stomach disappears, and the sinking feeling in my gut is gone. In that moment, all I want to do is run around the house and jump for joy. A huge, lopsided grin spreads across my face.

Cat, we need each other, I tell myself as I start typing a response.

from: West Ryder <WestRyderIsPerfect@gmail.com>

to: Cat Davenport <IAmCatwoman@gmail.com>

subject: (no subject)

Your Highness,

I am sorry to hear that. I will be at my beheading tomorrow. But before I die, West would like to know: what does this mean for him? Will you two stay friends and let him move back into the

Chocolate Palace?

As soon as I send it, my fists clench. I half-expect her to say no, to say that this friendship is over and then never respond to me again

But she doesn't.

My email dings a minute later, and I click on it, swallowing hard. Cat's response is two words: *We'll see.*

Chapter 9

I don't talk to Cat after that. Instead, I close my computer, watch a victory episode of Law & Order, flail some more, and eventually make my way back up to my bedroom. I sit on the edge of my bed for a while, just staring out the window at the dried leaves swirling in the air and spiraling down to the ground below, thinking about Cat. I hope this means we can go back to being normal. I hope we can just stay best friends, and I'll have at least one constant left in my life.

But how do I tell? Am I just supposed to wait? I can't wait for Cat, I can't just wait and see.

I get up and walk to my window, pressing a sweaty hand to the cool glass. My eyes wander to the empty street in front of me. Neither cars nor people pass by my house, and it's not like I can blame them. Every house in my neighborhood is either falling apart or too small to fit a family of more than two, and some both. This area is not exactly a sight to see. In the distance I can see the tops of much larger, much nicer houses—Cat's neighborhood. For an instant, a pang of regret comes over me. I wish I could be there with her, laughing and debating about random things and having ice cream eating contests like we used to. But instead? I'm stuck here.

I try not to think about it.

Beyond Cat's neighborhood lies the lake she and I always used to go to, which is located off to the right side of town. The lake is about a quarter mile long with a small, one-house island located in its center, and its water shimmery and calm. Every week in the summer when I was kid, I used to kayak across the lake and out to that mini island with my mom and dad. Most of the time we capsized, or spent more energy into random splash wars than we did actual kayaking.

We used to have a competition to see who could kayak to the island first, and the winner would receive bragging rights until next time. They would also be called, "Your Highness" by the two losers, and let me tell you, it's pretty freaking awesome to be called "Your Highness" by your own parents, especially in public. So one can say I had some pretty serious drive to win.

The best part of the competition wasn't the prize, though, but how serious we were about it. We would trash talk each other, try to knock each other's kayaks overboard, and we seemed to find every possible way to beat out the others. I remember how Dad once capsized Mom's kayak with his paddle when they were racing to the island, and she totally flipped out at him, swam to catch up with his kayak, then pulled him from his seat and dragged him into the water with her. The two of them started fighting and laughing and splashing each other and I just kayaked by, smiling, not realizing how lucky I was to have my family so strong and intact, not realizing how all that love I felt at the time would only come back to haunt me.

I return to my bed, fighting back tears. I miss Mom. I miss Dad. But more than that, I miss us. I miss those simple times back on the lake, when we didn't need to worry about anything, when we could just enjoy each other's presence and that's all there was: enjoyment. No catch. No fear. No nothing but each other.

We were such a tight-knit family back then, and now we're nothing. It still doesn't feel real, honestly, like this is all some elaborate dream and we'll go back to being normal soon enough. But in my heart, I know that will never happen. It's as if the tighter we were, the harder we were ripped apart.

I don't want that to happen to Cat and me.

I remember what my mom once told me: "If you care about someone, no matter what, fight for her."

My fists clench, and I take in a long, deep breath.

I care about Cat.

I'm not going to sit around and hope an email has fixed all of our problems

I'm going to fight for her.

***

I don't know what I'm doing.

One second I'm standing in my bedroom, staring at my hands and telling myself that I need to fight for Cat before it's too late, and the next I find myself outside, my coat on, running down the street to god-knows-where. It takes me a few seconds to realize I'm heading to Cat's house, the one place where I can always go to, the one place where I'm always safe.

And I'm going back.

The air is thick and misty as I run, and the smell of fallen leaves is everywhere. I gulp in some fresh air, clearing my head. I try not to think about what a horrible idea this is or even what I'm going to say to Cat, because I know that no matter what, I have to see her again, know that I can't go without her any longer. It's only been a day away from her, but it feels like eternity has come and gone, like she ran off with a part of me and I need to get it back.

I need to get *her* back.

My legs carry me all the way there, and I slow my pace as I reach her house.

This late at night it's dark outside, really dark, but I can still see my surroundings clearly in the moonlight. The houses on her street form a neat line, each of them looking so perfectly white it's like they've never been used. Immediately, my gaze shifts to Cat's driveway. It's almost like instinct, but I just *know* she is there.

I shove my hands deep into my pockets and walk slowly toward the driveway. The darkness keeps me hidden most of the way, and slowly, the nerves sink back in. When I finally reach the driveway, the motion sensor lights go off, bathing the area in a bright yellowish light. I look around.

I find Cat crouching by the side of her Dad's Mercedes like she always is, focusing her gaze on the car door. A brush is in her hand as she applies a fresh coat of red paint to its side.

I stop walking, listening to the distant echo of my footfalls throughout the neighborhood. Cat is only a few feet in front of me, still painting away as if she isn't seeing me, but we both know she's aware of my presence. I take another breath. A cloud of freezing air forms in front of my face and dissolves into nothingness almost immediately. I don't realize how cold it is until now, and a shiver races down my spine.

Finally, Cat's eyes shift from the car to my face, and my breath completely catches. In only twenty-four hours, I managed to forget how beautiful she was. I shift uncomfortably on my feet as soon as the thought crosses my mind.

I can't be thinking that.

But yet, I am.

The whole neighborhood is deathly silent, like we're the only two people left in the world.

"Hi," I breathe.

She stares at me, those blue eyes shimmering in the moonlight. "Hi," is all she says back, the paint brush still clenched in her hand. I watch as beads of red slip from the end of the brush and seep onto the ground below, making an almost inaudible *pat, pat, pat.*

There's a long pause, and it's in that instant—that single, unsmiling, heartbreakingly empty breath—that I realize how far apart we've grown. I step forward and hesitate, unsure of what to say but sure I have to say it.

"I'm sorry," I whisper.

For a second, nothing happens. Cat just looks at me, letting her paintbrush slip from her fingers until it clatters onto the driveway below, sending drops of red paint everywhere. Then, as if on cue, she laughs—a total, pissed-off kind of laugh. "Wow, that was incredibly creative and impressive, West," she says absently. "I'm glad you know how to make a girl feel so special."

A twinge of hurt shoots through me, but I shake it off, because I deserved that.

I take another step forward. Cat's house sits to our right, and I'm distinctly aware of how dark it is—the only light is from the motion sensor, which illuminates her pale face. "You know I mean it."

"Do I?"

"You do," I say, inching ever closer.

She stands up now, kicking the paint bucket to the side. "Look, do you have anything else to say to me? Apology accepted. Whatever. Now get the hell out of here so I can work on the car, okay?"

I grit my teeth. Not the kind of reaction I was going for. "Cat, please—"

She rolls her eyes, looking annoyed. "Please what?"

"Please... I don't know. Please just don't leave, okay? I don't want you to... leave." I kick myself in the ankle. I sound like *such* an idiot.

"And why not?" Her hands are on her hips now, but her eyes look sharp, calculating, like there is a wrong answer to this question and she's seeing if I pick it.

I close my eyes. "You really want to know?"

"I do."

This time, I answer her clearly. I grip her arms with my hands and look deep into her eyes. I'm consciously aware of her warmth flooding into me, of the shudder that races down my spine as our skin meets. "Because I don't want you to go," I say so quietly I'm not even sure if she can hear. I feel my biceps flexing as I hold her, hold her and don't let go. "I need you." The words seem to echo around the silent neighborhood, dancing every which way as if to taunt me with their desperation.

I need you.

But it's true. It's so freaking true. I need her, and it's that simple. I need her there for me, I need her presence, her smile; she always knows what to say, and I need that too. Fuck love. Fuck all of this. We're best friends. I can't stay apart from her over something this stupid. She's too important to me for that.

As soon as the words leave my mouth, Cat's lips purse into a thin line, and I can't detect any emotion from her. God, she has a great poker face. But me? Not so much. I can feel the warmth settling on my cheeks already, and I know—just *know*—I'm blushing. And hard.

This near to me, I can feel Cat's body inching closer and closer to mine. I see her lips, open and soft, sliding in closer to my jaw... And that hyperawareness scares the hell out of me. I've never noticed these things before.

Finally, Cat opens her mouth to speak. "Interesting," is all she says.

My heart sinks. "Interesting?"

"Interesting," she confirms, forcing a slight nod.

Here and there crickets chirp behind us and I can hear the distant hum of a car on a nearby road somewhere. It's cold out, freezing cold, but my skin is so hot from being near Cat that I barely even register it. I release my grip on her arm, shaking my head. "That's it?"

"That's it."

I sigh. "What?" I mutter, because by the blankness of her face, the subtle, sharp edge to her words, I can tell she's angry. She has reason to be angry, dammit. I was an idiot. An *asshole*. Look where that got me.

"What do you mean, 'what?'"

"Are we seriously going to do this?"

"Do what?"

I laugh, annoyed, and throw my head back. "I deserved that."

"You did."

I kick the ground. "Dammit, Cat! Why are we treating each other like enemies? We aren't! We're best friends, but we just... I just..." I close my eyes, gathering the energy to continue. "I don't want us to turn out like this," I finally say.

Before I even realize what's happening, my fingers reach out and brush her arm. I feel the searing warmth of her skin, then a tingle down my spine, and something else too. Something... I jump back, not wanting to know what it was. I shudder, and she just sighs.

"Could you be any more obvious about it?" she says.

I open and close my mouth before saying, "Probably."

"You're an idiot," she says.

I force a laugh. "I know."

"I'm glad. I thought I was going to have to *explain* to you why, and you know how thick-headed you are." Then, she smiles to herself, a distant kind of smile that I can't possibly place. She shakes her head, and the look disappears in a flash. "But, at least, you're a cute idiot."

I let a little grin slip onto my lips. "I am?"

"Unfortunately, yes, you are. It's just about the only thing you have going for you at this point."

"Not true."

"*So* true."

I roll my eyes. A slight breeze whistles past us and I feel the goosebumps prickling across the skin on my arm. My eyes lock on hers. Suddenly, it's just Cat and me and nothing but darkness.

I shift my gaze to my feet. "I miss you," I whisper, letting the wind carry my words, because this close to her, I know she can hear me. I can feel her, can almost anticipate her touch, her smile, and I know from the bottom of my heart that I really *do* miss her.

"I miss you too," she says, her eyes so big and genuine. "But I also miss us. Us... before."

"I know." I find myself nodding. "Me too." Then, "Think we can go back to being friends?"

She hesitates. A look crosses her eyes—a glimmer of something that looks like... regret?—but it's gone the second it comes. "Yeah," she finally breathes, turning her head back to the car. "I... I can do that, I think."

The air is cool all around, but between us, with each other so close, it's all warmth.

"Good," I say. "That sounds... nice. Being best friends again is nice. But promise me you won't try anything?"

"Like what?" A devilish look flashes across her lips.

"You know the answer to that," I say, my lips curling. It feels good to be smiling with her again, like a weight I didn't even know I was holding has been lifted off my chest.

"I don't," she says, feigning innocence, but I can see the faint trace of a grin on her lips. "Enlighten me, West Ryder."

I laugh softly. "Well, when mommie and daddie love each other very much, they..."

"They what? They eat pizza together?"

"Yes, Cat Davenport, when mommie and daddie love each other very much they eat pizza together. It's very romantic."

"Knew it all along," Cat says proudly. I shoot her a look that reads, "You are so weird." She responds by ever-so-eloquently sticking her tongue out at me.

There's a pause. Something crashes in the house behind us, a falling lamp or a giant textbook knocked off a table or something. Out here, I feel nothing but calmness, though, and even with the racing of my heart, I know I can't feel anything but it when I'm around Cat.

"So," I say, holding out my hand. "Friends?"

For an instant, Cat just stares at my outstretched hand, and I feel more coolness rush all around me. I can even taste the dew in the air, feel the softness to the night sky. "Okay. Friends," Cat says after a while, and she shakes my hands.

She starts to turn away after that, whether to go to sleep or return to working on the car I do not know. I start to turn back, too, shoving my freezing hands into my pockets, but before I can move Cat spins back around. Without a moment's hesitation she leans into me, her lips hovering a millimeter from my ear, whispering, "We can be friends for now. But West Ryder, if you think this means I won't fight for you with every last breath I have, you're in for a hell of a surprise."

Then she lets her hand slip from my arm, spins back around, and heads inside.

I stand there for the longest time, just staring at the spot where she was standing. Her touch sends a tingling sensation up my arm, her words making my heart pound harder and harder. I feel it all, but I don't know what to do.

Then, through the darkness, I smile.

Chapter 10

The next few days roll by quickly, and I find myself more focused on school and my vlog than anything else. I post another video, this one about relationships and euphemisms (I even include "having chocolate" as a potential euphemism, no thanks to Cat.) Cat and I talk here and there, mostly short conversations in the hallway or during lunch about why Albert Einstein must love ice cream or her lecturing me on the origin of lettuce, but even so, everything still feels weird between us. Friendlier, yes, but not quite… normal.

When I lay eyes on her now, it's like I'm looking at her for the first time. I no longer see her as just my amazing and hilarious best friend who I can't possibly go without, but also as a normal girl with a great smile and an air about her that draws me in. I notice things, too. How her hair cascades down the back of her neck. The way her lips move when she talks. The light in her eyes, so gorgeous, like a sea of deep blue. How pretty she looks when she laughs.

I've never noticed that before. But now? Now it's as clear as low tide at a tropical ocean.

On top of it all, I've been worrying. Worrying that this whole "go back to being normal" thing won't work out, worrying that the mega awkwardness will blow up in our faces, worrying that Cat and I will only have another setback that sets us further and further apart.

But worse, I worry that I'm getting in too deep, that maybe, just maybe, I will fall for her—and that will be the end of everything else we have.

I hope like hell it doesn't happen.

Soon the days grow colder, shorter, and the perfect season of autumn slowly melts into winter.

Things with my dad aren't getting any better any time soon, but at least we still aren't arguing. I still feel the need to do something to fix our relationship, though, to not just sit on my hands and wait. But what else is there? Therapy? He would probably kick me out if I so much as bring it up.

I don't talk to Cat as much as I used to during these early winter days, either, but we do at least talk. We can even be completely normal on occasion, forgetting the awkward between us, and at this point, that's all I can ask for. Her. Her comfort. Her warmth.

Still, I miss her. I do. I really really do. I wish I could go back in time, before all this happened, before love screwed me over once again. I want to go back when everything was so safe, when I still had a best friend to count on.

Finally, in the middle of the night, I get a call from Cat. I'm dead asleep when my phone vibrates on my bedside table, so knocked out, in fact, that it takes several rings for me to even wake up. When I do, I scramble out of bed, fumble around for the phone, and click "TALK," nearly murdering my lamp and history textbook in the process.

"Hello?" I mutter, completely groggy, and slowly sink back into bed. I glance at the time—3:30 a.m. A sigh escapes me. I don't think there's a worse possible time to call someone.

"This better be important…" I mutter to myself.

"West," Cat says, and her voice is so clear and strong that it sounds like she's just slept a good twelve hours. I am not sure what universe she lives in, but I've decided if that's the case, either she's insane or nocturnal. Probably both.

I collapse back onto my pillow. "That's my name."

"It is."

"And you're calling at 3:30 in the morning… why?"

"Because I felt like it," she says simply.

"You woke me up because you felt like it?"

"I did."

I shake my head, closing my eyes and sinking back into the covers. I switch the phone to speaker and place it on my chest instead, so I can lean back as I talk. "Cat, you're amazing, but do you actually have something important to say? I'm a normal human being, believe it or not, and that means I like to sleep at three—"

"You missed 'fabulous,'" Cat cuts in. "I'm not *just* amazing. I'm also fabulous."

I roll my eyes even though she can't see me. I yawn loudly, and I'm sure I'm going to fall back asleep any second now.

"So let me get this straight," I say, taking another breath. "You're calling me at three-thirty because you feel like it? And also because you want to remind me how fabulous you are?"

"That's exactly it. Also, I'm glad you've come to understand the ways of my inner fabulousness."

"Cat," I mutter, rolling over onto my stomach. My eyelids grow heavier, and the reminder that I have to wake up for school in two and a half hours seems to make me even more exhausted. "I'm going to bed. I'll talk to you tomorrow. *Goodnight.*"

Cat doesn't respond after that, and I vaguely wonder if she's just calling to annoy me or is legitimately angry again or... something else. I don't the let the thought continue. Right now, I just need to sleep. We can talk again in the morning.

With that, I sit up and start to turn off my phone.

"Wait," Cat says suddenly, and I hear muffled cursing on her end of the phone like she already regrets it.

"Yes?"

She pauses, takes a deep breath. "That's not... the reason I'm calling."

"Then what is?" I don't mean for it to come across so flippantly, but I'm too tired to think of anything but sleep sleep sleeeeeeeeeeeeeeeep.

Her voice is quiet now, slow and easy. "You really want to know?"

"I guess?"

She hesitates, and I can just make out her muffled breathing as she contemplates whether whatever she's about to say will be worth it. I know because I do it too. Do it to her, all the damn time nowadays. "West..." she says, and I can practically feel her sitting next to me, her side pressed to mine, touching my arm and whispering into my ear. And strangely, I... like the idea.

I scrub the thought out of my head the instant it comes up. I can't be attracted to Cat. Wait, no. I am *not* attracted to Cat. End of story.

"West," Cat says, more softly this time, "I'm calling you at three-thirty in the morning on a Thursday because I want to hear your voice."

That shuts me up.

In an instant, all of the exhaustion seems to rush out of me. I sit up, pressing the phone closer to my ear. My heart is pounding now, and I feel something inside of me grow, something light and buoyant. *I want to hear your voice*, she said. Oh my god oh my god oh my god. She wants to hear my voice!

I shake my head. Why do I care? Why does it matter that she likes talking to me? She's my best friend, so of course she does.

But the thing is, it *does* matter. It matters so much it scares me.

"I was lying on my bed because I couldn't sleep, and thinking about how I missed you and then I wanted to hear your voice," Cat continues. "So I called you."

Now my body really tightens. "You were thinking about me in bed?" I say, feeling a smile slip across my lips as I press the phone closer to my ear, wishing I could be sitting next to Cat right about now.

"Not in *that* way, perv," she says and laughs.

"Oh, shut up. It was *totally* meant that way."

"You flatter yourself. Unfortunately, you have no reason to." Then she adds, "I can feel you smirking through the phone."

"Dude, I so am not."

"You always were a terrible liar."

"Am not."

"Am too."

I grin. "Idiot."

"Loser."

"Freak."

"Creepo."

"Did you really just call me a 'creepo?'"

"Oh, West Ryder, I totally did."

I sit up a little straighter. "I have just lost all respect for you."

She laughs, and I swear I can feel her smiling through the phone, too. "Lies. LIES. All of them!"

"Sure," I mumble. A sliver of light peeping in from under the doorway illuminates some of my room, showing the outline of my small desk in the corner and my backpack sitting with my camera atop it. My dad snores in the other room, deep and gruff noises that bring a shiver down my spine. I sigh.

"But yeah," I say, nodding to myself. "I... I guess I miss your voice too. *As a friend*, that is."

"I think we've established that we're both friends here."

"I don't think we have," I say.

"Oh really? Still afraid I'm going to pull something, are we?"

"More like straight-up afraid of *you*."

"Oh yeah, at six inches shorter than you I'm utterly terrifying."

"You are! You know where I sleep. You could murder me. I wouldn't be surprised, either. Serial killers are always red-heads."

"And rapists are always blond."

I scoff, feigning hurt. "That's entirely inaccurate. Blonds are the gorgeous swimsuit models who all the girls drool over."

"Really? All the girls? Yeah, because I'm sure you get a ton of them."

"Yes I do. In fact, one is sleeping beside me right now. Isn't that right, Kayla?" I say to the empty space beside me, grinning like an idiot.

Cat cracks up. "Kayla? Kayla?! Oh my god what even goes on in your head?"

"An unending party."

"Of suck."

"I believe it is pronounced 'awesome.'"

"I believe you are mistaken."

"Oh, yeah, well... YOUR FACE."

"IS GORGEOUS."

"No."

"Yes."

"Idiot."

"Loser."

"Freak."

"Bully."

Cat sighs at that, and I can almost detect the happy smile

behind it, which makes a smile ebb at the corners of my own lips. I realize then how good it feels to talk to her again—like normal friends. To smile and not worry about loving each other, about drifting apart, about our friendship falling to pieces. Somehow, talking to Cat always seems to boost my mood, even at freaking three-thirty in the morning.

My eyelids start to feel heavy again, and I realize once again that I need to sleep. But a much larger part of me wants to keep talking to Cat, because sitting here, alone in the darkness and hearing her voice, I feel like I'm walking on air. I need Cat like I need to breathe, and that is that.

After a while, I glance around. My room is a mess of computer and camera supplies for my vlog, unfolded laundry, and some hardcore food-related posters hanging on my fading, blue-painted wall. My desk and bedside table sit on either side of my bed, shoved into the corner of the room, and aside from the closet in front of me and the window to my left, there is nothing else to it.

"So," Cat says after a long pause. I keep the phone pressed to my chest like it's some kind of sacred object I can't possibly lose. In a way, maybe it is a sacred object—after all, it's Cat on the other end and she is more sacred to me than anything else in the world. "I was thinking about going to the lake this weekend. You want to come, *friend*?"

"The lake?" I say skeptically.

"Yep. The one on the edge of town. It's only a few minutes away. You know it."

"I do," I say quietly. "We used to go there all the time." And we did—in addition to my mom and dad's kayaking wars, Cat and I used to go there too. We would sprint down the boardwalk and play in the water, running and jumping and having some seriously epic noodle wars, not even caring about the amused and slightly creepy adults watching us from the neighboring areas, and not even caring how utterly stupid we looked. Mom used to join Cat and I, to watch the sunset from the lake on some nights in the summer, and occasionally Dad would even join us too. Mom would always say that the sunset was the most beautiful thing in the world, that it symbolized rebirth and the beauty of coming back from adversity stronger and more competent than before and other things I can't possibly remember. We would sit on the edge of the lake, letting the water lap at our toes as we watched the sky turn red, yellow, orange, and then slowly into nothing.

I miss then.

I want then back.

"And… why do you want to go to the lake?" I ask Cat suspiciously. Lakes are not exactly romance-free places.

"Well, we're friends, aren't we?"

"We are."

"And friends tend to do things—like, be social."

"Okay," I say. "I'm with you."

"So. Let's be social. Together. Like normal humans."

I sigh. "Fine, fine. I'll go with you. But promise you won't pull anything, okay?"

"Didn't I already make this promise?"

"Yes. Now make it again."

I can almost feel her roll her eyes through the phone. "Yes," she says. "I, Cat Davenport, solemnly swear not to pull anything."

"Okay," I say. "Let's go to the lake together. As friends."

"For real?"

"For real."

"Well in that case, get ready for me to rock your world."

I don't bother holding back my smile. "I thought you said you weren't going to pull anything?"

"Oh West, you naïve little creature. I lied."

Chapter 11

I can't believe I let Cat drag me to the lake. I mean, it's Cat.

Clearly she is planning something, something more—well—intimate

than just a harmless visit to the water. After all, she herself said she is

going to fight for me. And yet, for some reason, I still find myself

wanting to go.

I try not to think about what that means.

I know it's a mistake, however, the second I get into Cat's

pickup truck and she speeds all the across town to the lake, nearly

killing several old ladies, a mailbox, and us in the process. When she

finally skids into the small parking area overlooking the water, the car

is moving so fast that I half-expect her to drive all the way through it

and plunge us into the lake. Admittedly, I'm surprised when she

doesn't. I grip my seat hard as she swerves in, does a dramatic U-

turn, and hits the brakes at the last second, causing the truck to jump up violently before it settles into parked position. My heart is in my throat at this point, and I turn to her, wide-eyed.

"I forgot what a terrible driver you are," I say, taking a breath of relief. I'm actually surprised I'm still alive.

Cat raises her eyebrow, giving me her "oh, no you didn't" look. "Please. I'm a badass driver."

"You almost killed an old lady on the way over!"

She shrugs. "The woman had it coming," she says like it's nothing.

I suppress a laugh. Sunlight floods in through the car window, warming my back, my legs, my stomach. I turn to Cat, unintentionally noticing how her skin seems to glow in the sunlight. It's warm out, really warm for a winter day, and her red hair looks so suddenly perfect on her shoulders. I take her in, bit by bit, my breath catching.

I should be used to looking her. Wait, I *am* used to looking at her. So why does she appear so different now? Why does it feel like, for the first time, I'm seeing what's really there?

I shake my head. No. *No.* This is not happening. We're friends. That's it.

"One day," I say to her, "I'm going to call you cupcake." The words roll off my lips before I can stop them, and I regret saying it instantly.

Cat pushes open the driver door and turns to me, narrowing her eyes. I glance out at the rest of the small parking lot. Aside from an abandoned SUV, we're the only ones here. "Cupcake?" she says suspiciously.

"For your red velvet hair. What? Would you prefer to be called 'red velvet?'"

"Yes."

"Okay, Red Velvet."

Cat frowns at me. "That's… entirely not romantic."

"Of course it isn't. We're friends, remember? Friends *aren't* romantic."

"Right," she says, giving an awkward nod. "Friends."

I roll my eyes. "You really couldn't make this weirder, could you?"

Cat doesn't answer right away. Instead, she shoves her foot against the door and lets it swing open. More light pours into the car as she steps out, turns back, and smiles at me. "For the record, West: I so can." And by the devilish glint in her eyes, I know she isn't lying.

With a sigh, I push open the passenger car door and hop out, only to be blinded by the sunlight, and follow her across the lot toward the lake entrance. There are no trees anywhere here, just a dirt parking lot and a crumbling staircase that leads to the lake below. Cat walks briskly, not even looking at me, and I have to jog to keep up with her. Dust flies up from under my feet as I move, and I can feel the breeze bat it back after me. I follow Cat down the stairs, then the next pair, then the next, until she stops so suddenly toward the bottom that I almost run into her.

"What—" I start to say, wondering what exactly has gotten into her this time, but then I follow her gaze out to the lake before us. I can't help myself; I gasp. But, I mean, it's beautiful. Like, actually beautiful. The water is so glass-like, shimmering under the bright sunlight, barely even ruffled by the breeze. Behind it, halfway across the lake, lies a distant island my parents and I used as our kayak race destination. A few boats surge through the vast of expanse of lake here and there, and I can hear the distant sounds of kids laughing and playing, the barking of a dog, the sound of water lapping against the shore. It's all so peaceful. So perfect. I turn to Cat, but her gaze is still focused on the water. The hot air warms my skin, making me shiver in a good kind of way, and I finding myself smiling. It's good to be here again. With Cat. Like old times.

I realize then that no one else is on our part of the lake, which is really just a patch of twenty feet of rocky land and a beach chair positioned in front of the water.

It's just us.

On the most beautiful day of the year.

Alone.

Warm.

Lonely.

My heart stops. Oh my god. Cat planned this all, didn't she? This whole setting, this complete perfection, was her idea? And she is a romantic genius, too. Oh shit. She knows my weakness.

As if on cue, Cat hops off the last staircase and onto the rocky shore below. She turns back to me after a second. I feel myself sweating under my "I SUPPORT RIGHTS FOR CHOCOLATE CAKE" t-shirt, because of Cat or the heat or possibly both I do not know. I go with the heat.

"So," Cat finally says, reaching for a rock on the ground.

I try to hide my nerves, not wanting to know what she is planning next. "So?" I say with attempted calmness.

She stares at me like I'm an idiot. "We're at the lake. It's hot out. Let's go for a swim."

My gaze shifts to my feet. "Oh…"

When I don't look excited, she edges closer to me, frowning. I watch, unmoving, as she looks me up and down as if trying to determine what my deal is. Then a light bulb seems to go off in her head. "Oh my god," she says. My breath catches. "Please don't tell me you're too scared to swim with me."

I shake my head. "No, I…"

Her hands are on her hips. Again. "Then what?"

"Nothing."

"You sure?"

"I'm sure." I'm not.

"Good," Cat says. "Then let's swim." At that, she turns and walks back over to the beach chair. I follow her, taking a tentative step off the stairs and onto the tiny strip of land we're on in front of the lake. Water laps at the shore, sweeping up some gray and brown rocks nestled in its path, and the sunlight seems to follow me everywhere. It's good, though—a refreshing change from the freezing winter nights.

I watch as Cat drops her bag off on the old, rickety beach chair, shakes her long hair, and reaches for her shirt collar. Then, without a moment's hesitation, she pulls it upward. It takes me a second to realize she's taking off her shirt.

My whole body freezes up. "What are you doing?" I say quickly. All the alarms in my brain seem to go off at once, like special Cat Trigger Warnings that are telling me this is not good. Not good at all.

It's not that I've never seen Cat in her bra before—I have on multiple occasions—but now it feels… different. Wrong, even.

She stops what she's doing and turns to me. "I'm taking off my shirt," she says blankly. "It's what people tend to do at beaches when they go swimming." I open my mouth to argue, but really what am I going to say? There is no argument here, so I clamp it immediately shut. My heart has started up again, and my breathing comes in rapid fire. Cat looks into my eyes. My jaw tightens. "Holy shit, West. You're scared of seeing me in my bra, aren't you?" she exclaims like she's just won some prize.

"No!" I say, shaking my head and blushing madly. She's totally right, though. "It's not..." I murmur. "No. *No*."

Wow. I don't remember being this un-smooth.

"Well," Cat says, still smiling, "sorry to disappoint, but this is just a bathing suit."

I blush even harder. "A bathing suit?"

"A bathing suit."

I glance at my feet. "Oh..."

Cat sighs. "Can I take off my shirt now so we can swim or are you still too terrified to see me without it on?"

"Yeah… okay. Fine. You're way too amused by this," I add, forcing a smile.

She throws up her hands. "Guilty as charged."

After a second, she turns back around. She drops her gaze to her shirt again, grabs the collar, and starts to pull it over her head. The fabric makes a slight swishing sound as it slides over her body, revealing a slice of lightly tanned stomach. I try to look away—I try, I really do—but for some reason, I can't. My eyes won't let me. So I watch as her shirt comes off, as it brushes against her body, slides across her shoulders and over her head, and suddenly she's wearing nothing but a bathing-suit-bra and jeans.

I hold my breath.

Her pants come off next. (I feel dirty just saying that.) After she places her shirt by her towel on the beach chair, she turns back to the water. She doesn't look at me as, ever so slowly, she presses her chin to her collarbone and reaches for her jean zipper. My skin crawls as the zipper slides slowly down, and I feel my face heating by the second. But I can't look away. I don't *want* to look away. I stare at her, the hot sun on my back, as she slides her jeans down her legs and off her body and places them in a neat pile next to her shirt.

Just like that, she's wearing nothing but her swimsuit. I stare, my eyes wide, unable to look away. I swear to you, two-piece bikinis will be the death of me.

Cat smiles shyly, glancing at her feet and blushing. I'm still staring at her and not even hiding my incredulity. Cat just did that. Took off her clothes in front of me.

Holy shit.

Then, an alarming thought strikes me: why can't I look away? Does that mean…?

I don't let myself answer the question.

"Now you," Cat says, glancing back up at me.

That snaps me back into reality. "Wait, what?" I say. "What do you mean?" My stomach sinks, and all of a sudden, I'm back on edge.

She rolls her eyes. "*I mean*, now it's your turn to take off your shirt."

A knot tightens in my stomach. "But—" I start to say, my mind racing to find an excuse, to think of *anything* to stop this.

"But? We're swimming, West. No one wears clothes when they're swimming."

I raise my eyebrow at that. Wait, does she mean…

"No one wears *shirts*, I mean. Jeez, you perv," she says. Then, Cat's lips break into a smile and so do mine. Relief washes over me.

"Whatever," I mumble. "It's cold. I don't want to take off my shirt…"

For an instant, nothing happens. Cat just stares at me blankly, and no matter how hard I try I can't read her expression.

Then, without warning, she breaks into a fit of full-on, amused, in-my-face laughter. "It's cold? Dude, you're sweating all over. There is no way in hell you're too cold right now." My face flushes harder as I glance back down at my shirt. She's right. I *am* sweating all over. I hadn't even realized, and now I need a new excuse. "I think you're just scared of my hotness," Cat adds.

"That's so not it. Actually, that's probably the last possible reason. I just... I don't want to this time, I guess."

"Like I'm going to believe that."

"It's true!"

"Wimp," she says.

"Jerk."

"Freak."

"Bully."

Cat shakes her head, suppressing a smile. A few birds fly overhead, and I can hear more splashes somewhere across the lake from people playing, laughing and shouting and being normal, like I wish I could be. "What? Do you need me to take your shirt off *for you*?" Cat says, still way too amused.

Okay. I think my jaw seriously drops here. "No, no," I say quickly, jerking my head from side-to-side. "That's not—"

But Cat isn't even listening. She's already stepped forward, her body inches from mine. "Here," she says, reaching for my T-shirt. "I got it." I don't even realize what she's doing until her fingers wrap around the collar of my shirt and she starts to pull upward. My whole body stiffens, and I feel a million tiny kinds of shock, confusion, and—horrifying enough—excitement wash over me.

Her stomach is pressed against mine, and I can smell her breath, feel her warmth, the overwhelming rush of our closeness. Her fingers work effortlessly, gliding my thin shirt along my stomach, my chest, then over my head. I shiver hard, my whole head a mess of emotions and warnings tangled with desire. For an instant, our eyes lock. She stares at me, hard and strong. I look away immediately, but I can't hide the blush—or the smile. My whole body feels on fire, and I don't want her to stop. She keeps dragging my shirt over my head, her thighs touching my thighs, her lips hovering a millimeter away from my own.

I stand there, unmoving, my jaw tight, my skin so hot and cold all at once. Finally, as she tugs the last bit of my shirt off my body, her finger brushes against the hardness my stomach for one beautiful instant, and then she lets go altogether as the shirt comes off. Cat steps back.

My whole body tingles, and I know it's wrong, but I already miss her touch.

When she finishes, I let out a breath and proceed to gulp in more fresh air. When did it get so freaking hot? Because that's all I feel now: hot. Burning, actually—still on fire from Cat's touch.

She folds my shirt perfectly and holds it out for me. All she says is, "Done" as she hands it to me. I give a slight nod. "Um, thanks. You, uh… are good at taking shirts off," I say, then want to kick myself the second the words roll out of my mouth. What the hell? 'Good at taking shirts off?' Who says that?!

Oh my god, I am such an idiot…

Cat raises her eyebrow and laughs far too loudly. "Wow, that was... smooth."

My cheeks feel hot all over again. "Yeah, um, anyway..."

"Yes. *Anyway*. We still need to take care of your shorts."

It takes me a minute to realize what she means by "take care of."

"Oh! Oh no," I say, narrowing my eyebrows at her. "No no no. I'm swimming in my shorts. There is *no way* I'm letting you do that."

She grins. "I know, and that's fine for now." She leans in and whispers, "But I assure you, West Ryder, when I'm done with you, those pants will go flying off."

Chapter 12

We head to the water a few minutes later. I gasp in a few more strangled breaths of fresh air as if it will somehow help me come to my senses with what just happened. Heat lingers on my face, on my skin, and I feel so buoyant again, so light and giddy.

Cat grabs two beach towels, hands one to me, and we walk down the small boardwalk until we reach the edge and are standing over about six feet deep of lake. The sun is still as strong as it was before, although the breeze has picked up again and the shrieking kids to our right have gone inside.

Sunlight pours its way onto my bare skin, and I shift uncomfortably beside Cat. I'm consciously aware that both of us are half-naked now. We've been here, at the lake, so many times before, done this almost every week for the past six months, but it's different now. Everything is different now. It's like Cat and I are new people, with new feelings and new…

I turn back to her to keep from finishing the thought. She's dressed in her red-and-blue bikini and I am wearing nothing but a pair of basketball shorts, and I realize this is exactly what she had planned.

Talk about manipulative.

"Staring again?" Cat says, biting her lip as she catches my gaze.

"Nope. Just looking out at the water."

"Liar."

I shrug. "If you say so." But really, we both know I'm lying.

"So," Cat continues, glancing down at the lake. "Who is going in first?"

"I volunteer you," I say.

She quirks her brow. "Really?"

"Really."

The water below is so clear and calm that I can see the rocks far below, but as I dip my finger in, I feel just how freezing it really is.

"Aren't you supposed to be the big strong guy who saves me and goes in first instead?" She laughs as soon as she says it. I shoot her a look. "Sorry," she says, holding up her hands, "I just can't call you 'big and strong' with a straight face."

I glare at her. "I'll have you know, I'm incredibly muscular. Girls practically cling to my side."

"Oh yeah?"

"Oh yeah."

"We'll see about that," she says, and before I realize what's going on, I feel a force at my side. The next thing I know Cat's hand is on my bare stomach as she shoves me off the boardwalk and deep into the water. For an instant, there is nothing but stillness and warmth from Cat's touch, and I feel like I'm hovering above the lake.

The next thing I know, though, I plummet to the ground. My body breaks the surface instantly, and all of a sudden, I'm submerged in six feet of ice-cold water. I sputter my way to the surface, laughing and gasping for breath, and a fit of shivers comes over me.

"You," I say to Cat, who is still standing on the boardwalk a few feet above. "You're done."

She sticks her tongue out at me. "Oh really?"

I take another breath, and the coolness of the water seems to wash away everything from before. Suddenly, it's just me and Cat, just two best friends playing at the lake like old times. "Yes really," I say. "You're coming in here with me."

I reach up a hand to pull her down after me, but she's already started running away, laughing and pointing at me and skidding down the boardwalk. My lips break into a smile, and with a grunt I pull myself up out of the water, swing my body onto the boardwalk, stand up, and chase after her.

"You'll never catch me!" Cat shouts, leaps off the boardwalk, and makes her way over to the beach chair.

A trail of water flies behind me as I maneuver after her. "Oh, Red Velvet, you innocent little thing. I am not leaving until you're as soaked as I am."

I leap off the boardwalk after Cat, whose blue eyes are wider and more full of life than I've seen in the longest time. I'm a few feet away from her now, so I lunge for her arm, but she's too fast. She wriggles past my grip, grinning like an idiot, and sprints in the opposite direction back down the boardwalk.

I smile, dip my head, and chase her.

"Aren't we not supposed to run on the boardwalk or something?" I call after her.

She doesn't turn back to me. "Screw it!" she says. "Society can suck it!" My grin spreads.

It takes another minute of running before she reaches the end of the boardwalk and turns around, nowhere to go.

"Well, well," I say, stepping toward her, more water dripping off my body. Cat stands only a few yards away from me, pinned against the end of the boardwalk, with nothing but me and the lake on either side of her. "I told you you're done for."

Her smile is so big it makes my heart seriously skip a beat. "I wouldn't be too sure," she says. "With your agility, you'll probably dive for me, miss, and fall into the water instead."

"Would you want to bet on that?" I edge even closer to her now. If I wanted to, I could reach out and touch her again, feel the awe-inspiring warmth of her skin on mine.

She tosses her red hair to the side. "Oh, believe me, I do."

"Good," I say softly, bending my knees and locking my eyes with hers. "Because I'm winning this round."

She lets out a shrill scream as I lunge at her, arms outstretched. My body flies into hers a second later, and my arms wrap around her waist as we plummet off the edge of the boardwalk and into the lake.

Together.

As one.

My arms are still around her even after we hit the water with a loud crack, and a shock of icy coldness comes over us. Finally, we break apart, Cat slipping out of my grip as she swims to the surface. Underwater, her hair streams everywhere, hitting my face and causing me to laugh. I swim up after her.

When we both break the surface, she giggles, gasping for air, and I smile between pants. "You asshole!" she screams and sends me a playful punch.

I laugh, wrapping my arms back around her almost instinctually. "Guilty as charged," I say. The sun has already begun warming us again, a stark contrast from the freezing water, and everything is so, *so* perfect. My smile keeps getting broader.

I'm still scared, though. Scared of how I keep feeling these things for Cat, keep wanting to touch her—scared of what it means. I mean, yeah, I'm not an idiot. I *know* what it means. But I don't want it to mean what it means. I want to be Cat's friend and only her friend. If I fall for her, there's a good chance we'll both fuck it up and even better chance we'll split apart for good. I care about her too much to let her go that easily, to risk losing her because of some stupid mix of emotions that I myself don't even understand.

I turn back to Cat. She is watching me as she bobs in the water at my side, but that smile of hers does not falter. Her hair is soaked and she looks like she's going to yell at me, and I just watch her, suppressing a laugh. "Idiot! You are an idiot!" she screams.

"Really? Like when I do this?" I bring my hands down on the lake, sending a thick spray of water right into her face.

She gasps and holds out her hands, looking entirely shocked and annoyed, her whole body soaked and dripping, and I think I've gone too far. But slowly, her lips part back into a smile. "Oh, West Ryder, you are so dead!"

The next thing I know Cat brings her hands down on the lake, too, and a flurry of water washes over me too. The cold spray only manages to send more and more energy through my body, though. I turn to Cat slowly, eyes locked, and I grin. "You're right, for once, Davenport. It. Is. On," I say and begin splashing at her rapid-fire.

"Oh yes it is," Cat shouts. She fights back, giggling hard, and soon we're both moving closer and closer in the water, splashing each other as hard as we possibly can. I'm soaked and blinded by the spray, the water in my ears, in my eyes, up my nose, but I don't even care. I just keep laughing and attacking until gradually, we're only inches apart and still dumping water over each other's heads, in addition to making quite horrible attempts at trash talk.

"West," she says some twenty minutes later, panting hard. We're both up to our necks in lake water, just swimming back and forth and making weird jokes and, for the first time since I found out Cat was Harper, being happy around each other. The smell of dried leaves is everywhere, and the air tastes like lilacs. The sky starts to gray as the sun sets in the distance. "West, can we talk?" Cat finally says.

"Yeah…" I say cautiously, frowning, because she sounds serious all of a sudden—too serious. "Why don't we get out of the water first?"

"Yeah." She nods. "Sure."

I climb out before her, pulling myself all the way up from the water to the boardwalk several feet above. I am consciously aware of her eyes on my biceps as I lift myself up, of the small smile that flickers across her lips when they flex from effort. She tries hiding it, but it's not something I miss.

And as I stand up on the boardwalk, my back to her, I find myself smiling too.

Cat takes the ladder up, flops onto the wood, and sighs. She sits in front of me, her legs crossed, her arms folded and her eyes trained on me. I still don't have a shirt on, and she's still wearing her bikini. Both of us are soaked, water dripping from our hair. She looks good like that, though—really good. I find myself noticing how soft her lips look this close to me, how it would feel to kiss the water off of them, what it would be like for them to move with mine...

I shake my head. *No.* This is the last thing I should be thinking about.

"Hey, West?" Cat says quietly, looking up at me with those big blue eyes of hers. Her face is tired, nervous, and by the sadness in her expression, I know immediately what she's about to say.

I tense up. "Yeah?"

"You know how I said I'm going to fight for you with every last breath I have?"

I look up at her, and she back at me. Her expression is hard, serious. "Yeah," I say softly. "I know."

"I mean it," Cat says. "I'm going to fight for us—first our friendship and then our..." She trails off, turning away.

"Our what?" I don't mean to sound so angry, but I can't help myself. Why the hell can't we just stay friends? Why does it need to be a real romance? Isn't the fact that we're with each other what really matters? It's not that I dislike the idea of going out with Cat; it's just that I'm not even sure *what* I feel for her. And until I'm sure, there is no way in hell I'm risking this not working and me losing her for good.

"Our..." She sighs. "Our potential to be more than just friends, I guess?" She winces at her words.

I want to punch something. I thought we were finally getting away from this weirdness.

"What's the matter, West?" she asks. I'm not exactly working to hide the annoyance on my features.

"You don't get it, do you?" I say.

"Get what?"

"Get us," I say, squeezing my eyes shut as if it'll help make this all go away. "You don't get that our friendship is more powerful than any romance will ever be. You don't get that we aren't 'just friends' but like siblings, that we were made for each other—maybe in the romantic sense, maybe not. But the thing is, it doesn't matter. I would be miserable without you, Cat. Hell, I'd probably be dead without you. But I'm not. I'm not because you're there for me. Because I can lean on your shoulder and you can lean on mine, because I can trust you, I can share anything with you, because I can love you however the fuck I want and it doesn't matter. We're lucky, you and I. Not many people have what we have. So, please, for the love of god, don't call us 'just friends' and act like we are nothing if we don't love each other."

I take a long breath as soon as the words roll out of my mouth. A long silence follows, and Cat just looks at her hands, saying nothing.

A part of me feels immediately guilty, like I've just committed some sin I can never take back, but a much larger half of me is glad to get it out, to finally say what I've been thinking since that first day I learned Cat was really Harper.

I drop my gaze to Cat's hand as she plays with the wood of the boardwalk, fingering its soaking edge. She doesn't say anything, doesn't even move, and I feel like an eternity passes between us right then and there.

I close my eyes. My pulse is pounding and my head throbs, and I don't know what I want anymore but I know it involves Cat—no matter what.

Always and forever.

Finally, Cat looks up at me. Her eyes are unsparkling, and her voice is soft, weak. "I get that, West, and that's what *you* don't get: that I get that. But the problem is," she says softly, "I fell in love with you, and that changed everything."

I can't look at her anymore. My heart thrums faster, faster, faster, and the sky above us slowly melts from a light gray to a dark blue color. The waves below continue to lap at the shore, and I can smell a barbecue coming from somewhere down the lake. "It doesn't change anything, Cat," I say. "It doesn't matter! We're still friends. We'll always be friends. Fuck, if you love me then go ahead and love me, but why do I need to love you back? Why do we need to love each other? Why can't we just stay normal best friends and be with each other like that forever? It's no different! I for one am not going to risk losing you for some fucked up set of emotions I don't even understand yet. So yes, I'm angry, and no, I'm not confused, and yes, I'm entirely freaking depressed but does that matter? NO."

My words seem to echo around us as soon as I finish, and my whole body starts trembling. I just want to leave. Everything seems to crash down on me at once all over again, and it strikes me then that no matter, we can never, *ever* go back to being truly normal. I choke back tears. My face feels so hot, and all I want to do is stand up and run and hide and never come back.

Cat reaches out to touch me, shaking her head, but I push her hand away. "Stop," I say, and she jerks away like she's been slapped.

"West, you're right," Cat whispers. "We *are* best friends. We *are* brother and sister, or whatever you want to call it, and we always will be. But that doesn't mean we can't try to be something else too. That doesn't mean we can't love each other." She shifts closer, starting to stand up now. "But let me tell you, West, no matter what happens, no matter where you go, I will also always be in love with you. And you don't have to love me back. Hell, you don't need to ever talk to me again. Will I be hurt? Yes. Will I want you back? Yes. But it will all still be worth it, because *you* have made it worth it. Because *loving you* has made it worth it."

Without another word, she stands up, walks across the boardwalk, gathers her clothes, and disappears out of sight.

I find myself sitting there, alone on the boardwalk, staring out at the vast expanse of lake with no idea what to do next.

Chapter 13

I trudge home after that, kicking random rocks as I go, feeling utterly miserable and empty inside. Cat drove off without me, so I walk the distance across town by myself. I keep my head down and my face blank, and the whole way, all I want to do is collapse in a heap and hope everything will magically get better. It's night out, and the sounds of passing cars and hooting owls keep me from going crazy as I keep on walking.

When I get home, I don't say a word. I just look at my dad, who's still sitting in his usual spot in the kitchen and head up the stairs without eating dinner, take a shower, and go straight to bed.

The rest of the weekend passes in a blur. I stay in my room the whole time, lying in bed and watching TV on my phone, only leaving to use the bathroom and eat. When Monday rolls in, I spend it entirely depressed. I don't talk to anyone, don't vlog, don't pay attention to any of my classes, and I don't even run into Cat. I go straight home the second classes are over, lock myself in my room, do homework, and sleep some more. It's like that for almost the entire week, and I swear I haven't felt worse since Mom died. I feel so depressed, so tired, like I can't move, can't do anything; I only have the willpower to sit in the corner and cry.

I miss Cat. Five days have passed since I last saw her, and I miss her badly. I wish I could get the courage to talk to her again, but I can't and I don't think I ever will again. We're drifting apart, I've realized, and we have been ever since she first told me she loved me.

Maybe we weren't meant for each other after all.

Finally, on Friday, I have my first human interaction in almost a week, with no one other than my dad. As soon as I push open the front door on my way home from school, drop my backpack off, and start to head back upstairs to my Room o' Sorrow, Dad steps in front of me.

"What have you been doing?" he says in a low voice.

I sigh. Not this again. "Nothing."

"You've barely left your room, West."

"So nice of you to finally notice something about me," I mutter, trying to push past him. This is the absolute last thing I need right now.

He holds me back. "I'm being serious, West." His eyes lock with mine. "What is going on?"

I shake my head, forcing a laugh. "Wow, for a second there you had me fooled, old man. I almost believed that you actually cared about me."

My dad steps forward, gripping my arm tighter. I can smell the alcohol in his breath from here. "It's not an act," he says. "I *do* care about you."

"Really?"

"Really."

I glare at him. "You're an asshole," I say.

He bites his lips, and it looks like he's fighting back anger. I almost snicker. Clearly he doesn't care about me. He just needs me to do him a favor, as usual. "What?" I say to him, not bothering to hide the disgust in my voice. "What is it you want from me? Money? Dinner? Something else?"

"West," he says, exasperated. "I don't fucking want anything! I just want to be sure you're okay! Why don't you believe me?"

"Hmm," I say, pissed off now too. "Maybe because you've ignored me for the last year? Maybe because you haven't shown a hint that you so much as *care* about in the longest time? Maybe because you treat me like shit all day, every day? Oh wait," I say, laughing angrily. "I have an idea: maybe because you fucking killed my mother and never said anything about it?"

"I didn't kill her!" he screams, his eyes wild, and it looks like he's about to punch me. "I made a mistake, West! I made tons of fucking mistakes! I treated you like shit and I deserve all of this, but you look hurt and I want to make sure you're oka—"

I push away from him, grabbing my backpack and feeling the bile rising in my mouth. "Never talk to me again," I hiss. "You aren't even my father. Not anymore. Not anymore."

For an instant, a look crosses his face—a pang of inexplicably raw sadness and regret. It disappears as soon as it comes, though, and a dark look replaces his features. His eyes narrow, and his hands begin to shake like he's fighting the urge to lunge at me. "You're a fucking waste of space," he hisses, so seriously that it actually makes me shiver. "Get the hell out of here."

"So you can scream at the air to make your dinner next time and starve to death when it doesn't? Deal." My heart is racing. The blood pounds in my ears. I throw my backpack at him and start to head right back out the door, needing to get out before I explode from anger and all of the stress of the recent days.

"Good! Now go cry to that girlfriend of yours like a goddamn baby!" he screams.

Now I spin around. I can't stop myself. My fingers curl into a fist. "She's *not my girlfriend*." No one messes with Cat. Not even my asshole father can get away with that.

"Yeah, suuuure. I know you two have been getting it on!"

My blood boils. "Fuck you!" I yell. "She's my friend. My *best* friend. I guess you wouldn't know about that, though, seeing as you have no friends!" I storm across the room, barely resisting punching that smug smile off of his face right then and there, and swing open the door. "I hope you're fucking dead when I get back!" I scream and slam it shut behind me.

Then, I run.

I run and run and run until I can't run any longer.

It's late afternoon now, and the sun is just starting to set. All I feel is the cool wind against my skin and the anger boiling within me and I just need to get away, to escape all this. I sprint down the street, past the other tiny, falling-apart houses in my cramped neighborhood, down toward the town center. I'm running so fast, so furiously, that I barely even know where I'm going. I just keep pumping my arms and legs, moving faster and faster, because maybe if I run quickly enough I'll outrun all of this. Maybe everything will go back to normal. Maybe I'll be shocked back to that happy time before Dad stopped caring and before Mom died, when I still had my best friend and family and when all I did was laugh and smile and not worry about anything except for cars and school.

I keep moving, letting the wind clear my head of everything but Cat. I don't want her to go. I *don't*. I always thought I loved her like a sister, but do I really? I keep feeling these things for her, things that are certainly more than just friendly. Am in love with her? How would I know?

Seconds turn into minutes, streets turn into avenues, and before I know it I'm stopping, out of breath, in front of a dark field. I pant for a minute, surveying line after line of graves in front of me. Out of the corner of my eye, I glimpse the yellow, orange, and light red of the setting sun beyond them.

After a minute, I take a deep breath and start walking through the maze of graves. Every step, every turn, is natural now, and I don't even have to look to know I'm going in the right direction. After six months of visiting this cemetery I know the path to the grave by heart, like it's seared so deeply into me that it can never leave. I wouldn't be surprised if that were the case.

When I arrive, I stop, open and close my eyes, and look at it.

Mom's grave.

It's small and white marble, still covered by the roses I leave every week when I visit her. It's peaceful, though—unharmed and content, like I imagine she is now. Slowly, I reach out and touch the inscription.

Rose Mary Ryder

1970 – 2013

Beloved Mother, Wife, and Mega-Badass FIFA Player

May She Rest In Peace

I smile a little at it, one of those sad smiles you get when you're trying not to cry. Mom *was* a badass FIFA player, though, and she would always beat Cat and I at it. When she won, she would laugh and do her victory dance which was really just her doing that scooba move over and over again. She always cheated, too, and she had no shame in trying to slide tackle her opponent's players until they got seriously injured. She was one of those loud, always happy moms who would trash talk me and throw her controller and party when she won, and I'd just roll my eyes and laugh at her. In that far off time before he fell apart, Dad would join in too, and they'd both make fun of me and we'd joke and play, or sometimes Dad went to my side and we both worked as hard as we could to ensure Mom would lose. But she never did.

I sigh a little, and I feel the tears glistening in my eyes. It's been six goddamn months, and it still hurts each day she isn't here. I know it's stupid, but sometimes I find myself staring at the front door and wishing, *hoping* she'll be back, like she's just on a trip, like she'll return any day now to play more FIFA and to bring the normal Dad back with her and to make everything happy again. She never is, however, and each time I don't see her face at that door I feel like I'm finding out that she's really dead for the very first time—over and over again.

I run my finger down the tombstone, then brush the roses I left here with the side of my thumb. The air is thick and smells like an assortment of flowers, and as I breathe it in, I feel something in the pit of my stomach already begin to settle.

Mom's grave, which is surrounded by foot impressions from my previous visits, is my happy place. It's the one place where I feel safe, where I feel truly at home, and it's also all I have left of my mom. It's where everything changed and everything will, where I'm reminded that she isn't just on some trip—that she's dead and gone and there is no coming back.

Then, I can't take it anymore. Everything from this past week seems to catch up with me at once, and I bury my head in my hands and cry. I let the tears slip from my eyes and down my cheeks. They burn my skin and I don't even care, because crying, at least, means letting go. Means giving up and then fighting harder for what really matters, for what still can be fixed. I cry for my mom, my dad, for Harper and Cat. I cry because I need to cry, because it feels good to finally let out it all out. To finally face the truth.

And just like that, I long for Cat again. I long for her warm embrace, for her comfort, for *her*, really, and I don't even know what I'm doing but the next thing I know my phone is in my hand and I'm calling her.

My tears fall from my nose and splash onto the screen as the phone rings once, twice, three times, and I hold my breath, hoping she'll pick up, needing her to forgive me just one more time.

There's a click, and my whole heart seriously flutters.

"Hello?" Cat asks slowly, carefully.

"I need you," is all I can whisper out.

Chapter 14

Cat comes less than five minutes later. I don't even need to tell her where I am because she already knows. She gets me like that—inside and out—like I'm that crossword puzzle everyone knows the answer to. She pulls up in front of the cemetery in her red truck, jumps out, and runs over to me. The sun has almost fully set now, and the sky is a mixture of gray and orangey-yellow. It has started drizzling a little, and Cat throws on her hood as she rushes, head down, over to me.

I've stopped crying now, and I'm left fingering Mom's name on the inscription, *Rose Mary Rider*, until my thumb starts bleeding from rubbing it so much. Her mom named her that—Rose Mary. Like a rosemary, Mom said, which was the same flower her father gave to her mom the night he proposed, and the same one Mom gave to Dad on their wedding day.

I don't meet Cat's gaze as she stumbles over to me, crouches down at my side, and looks into my eyes. "Hey," she whispers slowly. Rain trickles down my face, washing away the tears and the screams and the pain. I just stare miserably at the gravestone, my shirt wet and clinging to my stomach and my hands shaking vaguely. "You okay?" Cat asks.

"No," I whisper. "I... I dunno. I'm just... lost."

She shifts closer. It's only a tiny, tiny movement, but I can't help but notice how her body creeps closer to mine. We're only an inch apart now, so close I can reach and touch her if I wanted to.

And I do want to.

"It's okay," she whispers.

"Is it?"

"Yes, West, of course it's okay. You have me, remember that. I'm here for you."

I shake my head. My eyes are still trained on the tombstone. "Even now?"

She places her hand on my shoulder, and her warmth sends a series of jolts throughout my body. I don't want her to stop, either. "Even now. I'm always here for you, West," she says quietly. "Always. No matter what."

My heart seriously skips a beat.

I'm always here for you. No matter what.

I'm not sure why, but her words keep echoing throughout my head. She's here for me. By my side. Hand on my shoulder. Thigh touching my thigh.

I want her.

I need her.

I... love her?

I can't find the words to respond, though, and the silence seems to stretch on for an eternity. More rain comes down, a little harder now, streaming down both Cat's face and my face.

"Remember," she says after a minute, her voice soft, and then she smiles to herself. "Remember when we were kids and we decided we were going to revolt against our teachers. So we planned to round up all of the other kids, supply them with orange juice weapons, and stage an attack?"

The smile grows. "Yeah. I remember."

She inches closer again, and I can feel her warmth, smell her vanilla scent wrap around me. I feel safe with her, like we're in our little world again, like nothing can hurt us when we're with each other. "It was a terrible, terrible plan," Cat continues, "and it's no wonder the op failed as soon as the lunch lady yelled at us for taking the orange juice grenades, but you know what I loved about it?" Finally, I turn to her. Rain streams down her face, wetting her red hair and dripping down her cheeks and off of her chin. I feel it on me too, all over now. I watch Cat's eyes on my shirt, her lips moving with every word. "I loved it," she whispers, "because I was with you."

There's a single moment that follows where neither of us speaks a word, just listen to the sound of the rain and lock eyes with each other. For the longest, most beautiful instant, we just stare. Unmoving. Unsmiling. Rain pouring down us—only with each other.

Then, without thinking, I reach out and push her wet hair to the side like I did so many nights ago, so I can see more of her beautiful face. And I'm right: it *is* beautiful. Heat creeps into Cat's features, and she drops her gaze back to her lap, looking so completely shy and vulnerable. "I know it's going to be okay," she continues, "because I still have you."

Then, ever so slowly, she places her left hand on my cheek. I don't flinch, don't even tear my gaze from hers. Her hand is warm at the touch, and I shiver a little bit as her skin brushes mine, but I don't tell her to stop, don't push her hand away. Weirdly, I don't *want* to push her hand away.

"I'm glad you came," I say quietly. "I... was an idiot, through all of this. I shouldn't have done that to you. You've always been there for me and the one time I should've been there for you, I wasn't." I move my face toward hers ever so slightly, close enough to feel her minty breath, to catch the rain streaming down between us. I whisper, "I'm sorry."

The sky is all gray now, and the rain is coming down hard. My white shirt is so wet I know she can see my stomach, the outline of my chest, and for some reason, I don't even care. I want her to see. I want her to move closer. I want...

What do I want? Her? Her touch? Her *lips*? She's my best friend. I'm not supposed to feel like this, but I do. Is this what Cat was talking about? Am I really falling in love with her, like she is falling in love with me?

A flicker of a smile crosses Cat's lips, but it's gone before I can figure out what it means. "You *were* an idiot," she says, and laughs a little. "But that's what I expect from teenage boys, I guess. You're all idiots on the outside."

I roll my eyes. "Whatever."

"It's the truth! Meanwhile, girls are fantastic."

"Indeed. Anything with breasts is fantastic."

Cat laughs. "Oh my god, West. Did you really just say that?! Jesus, you are so freaking weird…"

"And adorable?"

She shoots me a look. "Possibly."

I toss my hair, feigning confidence even though I feel so empty inside. "Red Velvet, I'm like a puppy. Lovable, fun, and *entirely* adorable."

She shakes her head, suppressing another laugh. "*Anyway.* You may be an idiot teenaged boy. But," she says, and drops her voice to a whisper, "on the inside, you are the most amazing, most resilient and carefree spirit I have ever met."

My heart races all over again. She says it so simply, so bluntly yet honestly, that I know she means it.

"And you," I whisper back, "are the strongest, coolest girl I've ever met, and the fact that you can deal with me, asshole-dom and all, and still see the goodness in me, means you are more clever, more intelligent, more *beautiful* of a spirit than anyone I have ever met."

Even more rain comes down, and another instant follows where we both look at each other, *really* look at each other, and wait. And wonder. I am consciously aware of her hand still on my face, of the rain running down my chin to her fingers, then off to the ground. The pattering sounds seem to fade, though, like background noise or something. My ears starting ringing and it's just the two of us, in our own little world, in our own little connection.

Then Cat tilts her mouth just a fraction of an inch to the side, a movement so subtle I almost miss it. But I don't. I focus on her lips now, on the rainwater slipping, so slowly, off of them, and before I know it, my lips are tilted too.

I lean in without thinking, slowly at first, hesitantly. She follows my lead, and in that instant our mouths are so close and still so far away, jerking forward a little and then back all over again. I hesitate there, not sure what to do, not sure whether to go through with this no matter how badly my heart and head and the rest of my body want it. I take a small breath, but it's enough to send a shiver of anticipation racing up my spine. In a rush, I move even closer until our lips hover only millimeters away from each other's. I close my eyes, my heart pounding, my skin all hot and cold and soaked from the rain, and I realize it would be so easy to press my lips to hers.

But I don't.

Before I know what's happening, I pull back just slightly, my hands shaking all over. For the longest time our lips hover there, begging to connect for real this time with the force of seventeen years of waiting, but I won't let them.

I pull away altogether.

When I do, Cat looks at me oddly, sad and understanding at the same time. I lock eyes with her and whisper, "Not now."

Then I stand up, and leave her alone in the pouring rain.

Chapter 15

The next few days rush by in a blur of pent-up emotion and total confusion. Exam prep hits me full force, and I spend most of my time studying and watching TV and doing everything I can not to think about Cat, or my dad, or any of this. Cat and I stay mostly normal, although we each conveniently refrain from mentioning the awkward-as-hell almost-kiss between us, but when I get free time, it's all I can think about: her lips. My lips.

At the time, our lips were like magnets. I wanted that kiss. I *needed* that kiss. But I pulled away.

I don't really know why I did what I did, but it just felt... wrong. I mean, I can't kiss Cat. Not like that, at least—not at Mom's grave and certainly not when I'm too busy suppressing tears to think clearly. If we kiss—and I'm not saying we will—I want it to be real. Honest. I want us both to be ready, and I want it to be the best damn kiss this world has ever seen.

But even so, a part of me regrets not going through with it. A part of me *wants* to see how a kiss with her feels, because maybe kissing Cat will tell me whether I really do love her. But I can't risk it. What if I feel nothing? We'll have kissed and then that will be that, and we can go ahead and forget about ever being ordinary friends again.

I haven't talked to Dad since our fight, but strangely, he wasn't angry when I got back. Instead he looked... sad. Regretful, even. But I know my dad and I know how good he is at pretending, and he is sure as hell not the type of person to be regretful. Mom's death is proof of that. Then again, he's also not the person to fight with me that hard. It almost feels like a relief to get something out of him, something beyond the zombie insults.

Cat and I don't have our first real conversation until a few days after that night. I mean, we talk a little here and there about the probability that our ancient History teacher lived when dinosaurs existed, but we've conveniently avoided the topic that is on both of our minds: the near kiss.

After school on Thursday, I throw my books into my locker, ready to go home to another uneventful night of avoiding my dad and Cat and filming another vlog, when I get her text.

It's me, Cat says.

Shocker.

Shut up. Also, meet me outside. I brought ice cream!

For real? Jeez, Cat, you sure know the way to a man's heart.

I know. I'm wonderful. You don't deserve me. But because I'm nice, you get to meet me outside.

I roll my eyes as I type, *Whatever.*

Don't "whatever" me, Ryder.

Oh, but I already did! Muahaha!

Do you want your ice cream or not?

I do.

Then come meet me outside.

FINE. No need to be so bossy.

Me? Bossy? No! I am sorry for whatever terrible thing happened to you as a child.

Yeah. I met you.

gasp Oh you did not just say that!

Oh yes I did!

I smile to myself, pocketing my phone. Talking to Cat never fails to make me feel so much better. When I've finished emptying my backpack, I slam my locker shut and walk down the hallway and out the door. I find Cat seated on a bench a few feet to the right of the school entrance. It's sunny out, way too sunny to be winter, and the air is cool and somewhat icy.

"Hey," Cat says. I turn to her. Her blue eyes sparkle in the sunlight, like hidden jewels only I know about. She holds her palm over her eyes and angles her head slightly to block the sun, so she can watch me approach. Her red hair spills over one half of her head, and her cheekbones stand out as she gives me a huge grin. Then I notice the ice creams sitting on the bench next to her.

I gasp, stick out one hand and hold the other to my chest, feigning a dramatic, soap-opera-esque moment. "Could that be... ice cream?"

"Why yes, yes it is."

"Vanilla?"

"With rainbow sprinkles."

I grin. "You really do know how to please a guy, Cat Davenport."

"Like hell I do."

I sit down next to her, taking one ice cream and handing the other to her. She gives me a spoon, says, "Enjoy! I'm a badass, I know," and for a little while, we just eat and stare out at the other students leaving school, at the sports teams getting together for practice, anything than to meet each other's gaze. Anything but to face the truth.

If there was a prize for most awkward maybe-couple, we would come in first.

"So," Cat says when we're both done with our (delicious) ice creams. "You ready for exams?"

"No. You?"

"Nah. I'm too busy buying ice cream for this friend of mine."

"You mean you're buying ice cream for other guys?" I say in my fake-dramatic voice.

"PLOT TWIST!!!!"

"You are such a dork."

"No, no," she says, shaking her head. "West Ryder, I am wonderful."

"Well, that may be true," I say, turning to her, "but you are still a dork. Correction: you are *my* dork."

"And you love me for it, right? For being a dork?" she says jokingly, but as soon as the words leave her mouth we both realize what she's just asked. She stops, holds her breath, and I feel like I've been slapped.

"I..." I say, not entirely sure how to respond. She raises her eyebrow. "Um, well, this is awkward," I finally say.

"I agree," Cat says, forcing a nervous laugh.

I listen to the hum of cars driving past, the distant chirping of birds in the trees high above. The sky is clear aside from a few clouds, and it feels nice to be outside with Cat again. "So, Cat," I finally say. "I don't really know what is going on... with... us... but I do know that whatever happens, I don't want to lose you. So for now, maybe we could try just staying best friends again?"

I am acutely aware of her eyes on me, studying me. There's a long silence before she answers. "Friends," she murmurs as if to test out the word. Then she starts nodding, and says "Friends" again, louder this time, and I know she's agreed. "Yeah, okay. That sounds good."

"You sure?"

"Yeah," she says.

"You always were a terrible liar."

She narrows her eyes, looking at me with both suspicion and curiosity. "Why do you think I'm lying?"

I smile vaguely. "Your lip," I say. "It always twitches when you lie. Just a little, but it's always there. It's been like that for years."

She moves closer to me, her side only inches from mine. "You were watching my lips?"

My stomach drops. Oh shit. I was, wasn't I? I was staring at her lips. It was so natural I didn't even notice it, but I still *was* staring at her. Whoa. "Yeah, I mean… no… I mean…" I trail off.

"You're also a terrible liar," she says quietly.

"And how do you know that?"

She nods at my cheek. "Your dimples. You always bring out the dimples—or as I like to call them, the Big Guns—when you lie, because you're so focused on looking normal and smiley and *not* like you're lying that you look exactly like you're lying."

I whistle to myself. My eyes are on hers. "So we can even tell when the other is lying," I say quietly. "We're like an old married couple and we aren't even a couple."

"Yeah," she says, "I guess." There's a pause, and we both look at each other, searching for words to say but coming up with nothing. "This is weird, you know. We're both skirting the whole romance thing, intentionally or not. We can't keep doing this, can we?" I don't respond.

"Either we try…" Cat takes a deep breath, hesitates. "…to be more than friends, or we stay best friends."

"It has to be so black and white?"

"I think so."

I close my eyes. "I guess… I guess we should stay best friends," I say. "If we have to choose."

"You sure?"

"I'm sure."

She nods reluctantly. "You're right. We'll be badass, ice-cream-eating best friends and forget everything else. Deal?" she asks.

"Deal," I say, but as soon as the words leave my mouth, I'm not sure I mean it.

Chapter 16

I spend the rest of my afternoon in my room, not studying, not working, just staring up at the ceiling and thinking.

Dad approached me on my way up the stairs nearly an hour ago. This time, though, he didn't glare at me, didn't scream about what a waste of space I am. He just said, "Hey," and his eyes were trained on mine, but he looked so suddenly tired, like the stress of the last year had finally hit him. I mumbled "Hey" back and slipped past, because I knew a conversation with Dad would only result in me feeling worse and worse, and I can't have that again. "Good luck with exams," Dad mumbled as I raced up the stairs. Then I heard him sigh to himself like he regretted something. He moved back to the kitchen. For more beer, I assumed.

As I lie there, I keep thinking about Cat, about Mom and Dad and our broken family. It shouldn't hurt this much, but it does. I mean, it's been a year with Dad how he is, half a year without Mom, and *I still have Cat*, so why does it matter anymore? I should be over it. I shouldn't be visiting Mom's grave every week hoping she'll return, I shouldn't be acting as if Dad is just a little tired and having 365 consecutive bad days, I shouldn't worry about whether I love my best friend or not. We're still friends. We fought, but she's still here. I don't need love to be happy. *I don't need to worry.*

Sometimes, like now, I wonder why Dad stopped caring. It feels like it's been a millennium since he was happy, but really it's only been a year. I guess I'll never know why he gave up, though. It's just one of those things that I don't really need an answer to. Maybe he got depressed. Maybe he let it get to him. Maybe work was too stressful. Maybe he just decided to call it quits.

I don't know.

And I'm not sure I care, either.

I sigh, click over to my vlog page, and refresh it aimlessly a few times, but I don't know what to think, what to *do*. Then I see my camera positioned in front of me. My camera. The only way I have ever been able to get my thoughts out before. It worked for Mom, kind of, so maybe it'll work now. For Cat. For Dad. I roll my eyes at how stupid it sounds, but it's not like I have anything better to do. So I reach out and turn on then camera, take a breath, and start talking.

"Sometimes," I say into the lens, "loving people sucks. It's scary, terrifying really, but you have to do it. You have to take that deep breath and make the plunge, for all of its hurt and emptiness and confusion to come, because loving someone is worth it. I loved my mom," I say, but I can't look at the camera any longer. Instead, I focus my gaze on my light-blue-painted wall in front of me. I keep blinking and blinking, hoping the tears won't come again. "She's gone now," I continue, "and now my dad is gone to me, too. It... hurts... to lose someone you love. When Mom died, I..." I close my eyes. Talk about making a fool of myself. "I didn't know what to do," I say, my voice hushed. "I felt empty, lost, hurt, and more than that, I felt confused. How could someone I love die on me like that? How could it hurt so much? And why couldn't I have had a warning? I mean, I never even got to say goodbye…" Another pained breath. The tears keep threatening to come, but I fight them. I'm not going to cry. I'm strong. I'm *strong*. "And then I couldn't stop wondering why the hell I bothered to love her in the first place, if all it did was leave me with tears and pain and a deep sense of confusion."

I grit my teeth.

"That was my low point. How could I forget all of the happiness she brought me when she was alive, just like that? How could it suddenly be not worth it? How could a moment of pain change how I feel about my own mother? I didn't know, and that was and still is the problem: I don't know. But," I say, "I wouldn't trade loving her for anything else. Sure, the memories don't turn into happiness as quickly as they say. Sure, you don't just 'get better' one morning. Sure, it feels like you're trapped and will never escape. But that doesn't matter. It feels like that because you've loved someone, and that's an amazing thing. That's something *important*. And yeah, it hurts. It fucking burns. "But," I say, "it hurts because it matters."

I pause, my temples pounding, my head throbbing so hard I swear it's about to explode. "There's this girl who I've known for the longest time who, the other month, told me she loves me. And now? Now I'm afraid of her. Afraid of wanting her. Afraid of *loving* her. But why? For what? Because I'll be broken again? Once again, I don't know. I don't know what's going on with me. I just know... that I don't want to put myself out there again. That I don't want to lose anyone else." I tighten my jaw. "But I'm done hiding. I'm done being afraid. So I'm taking the leap. Eventually, it will hurt. Eventually, I will fall off this cliff of happiness, at least for a while. And yes, it will feel like my heart is being ripped apart over again, but it won't even matter, because I will have been with her."

I close my eyes and look away, my whole body a mess of energy and mixed emotions. Then, without thinking, I turn off the camera, sync the recording to my computer, take a deep breath, and upload it.

***

"West!" Dad calls from downstairs a few minutes later.

"Dinner! Now!" I sigh and stand up. Time to make him dinner. Again. I

stumble down the stairs, my head throbbing, and turn into the

kitchen.

But this time, Dad isn't sitting on the table with his beer,

waiting for me to do all his work for him. In fact, all of the beers are

tucked in the corner of the room, near the recycling, and Dad is

standing in the kitchen, wearing Mom's old apron and holding up a

spatula. I stare at him, and he forces a small smile as he holds out a

piece of chicken.

"I made dinner," is all he says.

Chapter 17

It hits me the second I swing open the front door on my way back from school the next day. Cat's birthday. It's tomorrow.

Oh shit, oh shit, oh shit. It's really her birthday tomorrow, isn't it? And I forgot. I've been so focused on everything else that I completely forgot my best friend's birthday. I haven't even gotten her anything.

Yep. I'm officially the worst friend ever.

But after everything else I've screwed up, there is no way I'm ruining her birthday of all things.

In a flash, I throw my backpack inside, mumble to my dad that I'm going to get Cat a gift even though I know he can't hear me, turn, and run back out the door. I'm many things, but "poor present giver" is not one of them. I'm basically the king of presents, and I plan to stay that way.

I climb into Dad's old pickup truck, slam the door, turn on the ignition, and start driving. I almost hit our mailbox as I back out, but I don't care. I press my foot on the accelerator and speed down the road to the supermarket, because that's where all the true present-giving badasses go. One red light, one downed stop sign, and two near-dead old ladies later (I'm still not entirely sure how I passed the driver's test…) I skid into the grocery store parking lot.

"This'll be the best damn birthday present you've ever seen, Cat Davenport," I mutter to myself as I push open the door, step out of the car, and walk inside the store. The supermarket itself is less "super" than it is a market, with its mere four cramped aisles of food. At the very least, however, it has what I need. The lights flicker above me as I walk, and I appear to be the only customer in here aside from the creepy old man standing in the corner. I go for the cake supplies immediately. Cat loves cake almost as much as I love ice cream. But even more than that, she loves cake when someone bakes it *for her*. I remember how her face lit up last year, when I made her the most kickass Dora the Explorer cake known to man, how she shrieked and danced and grinned at me. Just the thought of her looking so happy brings a smile to my lips.

On top of the standard cake supplies I grab Oreos, chocolate icing, and a packet of sour gummy worms, her favorite toppings. I also slip in a bag of cookie dough for myself because hey, a guy's got to eat.

When I'm back home, I head to the kitchen, dump out the eggs and sugar and the rest of the groceries into a large white bowl, and begin my cake cooking expedition. Dad isn't in the kitchen for once, and that I am thankful for. He's probably passed out on the sofa in the family room, though, which is not exactly something I want to get myself into now. So I distract myself with cooking. Next I get out the butter, the Oreos, and start preparing the cake.

There is no way I'm screwing up Cat's birthday, too, I tell myself as I work. *There. Is. No. Way.*

It takes a few hours of cooking mastery before the cake is finally ready, but when it's done, the cake is, let's be honest here, fan-fucking-tastic. It's large, at least the size of my face, and it's smothered all over with dark chocolate icing. Above the icing is a layer of sour gummy worms, and on top of those, I make a mini Oreo pyramid.

But the cake is not done yet. The best birthday gifts are also sentimental, so I head back up the stairs to my room. Pictures, I tell myself. I need pictures. Old pictures of Cat and I, of us smiling and having a good time, of Cat doing weird things and me taking photos of it. I'll put them around the cake, on the plate, for her. When I reach my room I hear Dad muttering to himself in his own room across the way. For an instant, I strain to hear what he's saying, but I can't make out his words. I shake my head and shut my bedroom door. *It doesn't matter.* I go back to looking for pictures of Cat.

It takes me a minute of throwing around clothes and old trinkets before I find a photo album of us. I smile a little as I pull it out and open it up.

I flip through page after page of photos, starting with when Cat and I were kids and we went to the bus stop for the first time, to when we were six and lost our first teeth and showed off our gap-toothed smiles to the camera, to when we went skiing together in sixth grade and quickly learned we were *not* born skiiers. I pull out a few more pictures here and there, of Cat and me sticking out our tongues to the camera, posing in front of *The Icecreamery* as kids, and so on. Eventually, I make my way to the more recent pictures, smiling like an idiot all the way through. I feel something else, too, though; the beating of my heart. The buoyancy inside me. I look at the pictures of us, how close we were, how much we loved being around each other, and I start to feel... well...

I turn the page before I can finish the thought. These pictures are of Cat and me showing off our dorky Harry Potter Halloween outfits, Cat and me looking like Sumo Wrestlers as we joke-fight each other on the boardwalk by the lake, Cat holding my hand and telling me I'm the biggest badass of a friend anyone could ever ask for.

I flip the page. Next are pictures of us playing our epic games of whiffleball, which Cat always won, where we were laughing and smiling and not caring how stupid we looked. Another picture shows us on that trip to France we took with Mom last year, where we're wearing fake mustaches and French painter hats, posing for the camera and grinning so hard. The next shows me and Cat doing our best fish impressions at the beach, our faces inches apart, our lips puckered like a fish's. Then, I see one of Cat and me dressed up for our first Prom, our arms around each other, our faces so close and smiles so wide. By how happy we looked with each other, it seemed like we were going to Prom together, even though we went with different people.

I turn the page. My heart tingles, rising slowly upward in my chest. All of a sudden, I can't think straight. I've completely forgotten why I was even looking at these pictures in the first place, because now it's just Cat and me and our memories. And as I look at those pictures of us laughing and smiling and being dorks and not caring because we have each other, my eyes start to mist—and I just know.

I know like you know if you failed a Math test, or you did well in a job interview; I know because of that little instinct in the back of my mind screaming at me that "YES!! THIS IS THE RIGHT ANSWER!"

I know right then, as I stare at those pictures, that my quest for happiness, for *love*, was right in front of me the whole time.

I know that I, West Ryder, am in love with my best friend.

***

Before I realize what I'm doing, I bolt out of my bedroom, abandoning the cake and the photos and my dad and everything else, fly down the stairs, out the front door, and sprint faster than I ever have before to Cat's house. It isn't a long run, but I wouldn't have noticed if it were a thousand miles long because I can't stop smiling. My whole head is filled with Cat Cat Cat and me me me, and how did I not notice, how could I have missed that I'm in love with my best friend this whole time?

It's midnight, so I run in tune with the crickets chirping in the distance, smiling as the wind ruffles my hair. A few minutes later I arrive at her front door, panting like crazy, my whole body so light I might as well as be flying, my heart skittering in my chest.

I'm in love with Cat. I'm in love with my best friend.

Oh my god. Oh my god oh my god oh my god. This is really happening, isn't it? I'm really in love with her?

Cat opens the door a minute after I ring the doorbell, yawning a little.

She frowns when she lays eyes on me. "West? Everything okay? It's late."

I look at her. She's dressed in her Harry Potter pajamas and a pair of pink socks, and she holds her hands at her waist. Her hair is a mess, but it looks so adorable and perfect in its own little way. Dark circles surround her eyelids, but her blue eyes shine so brightly it still looks like she can take on anything.

"Yeah," I say, "everything's fine. Sorry to wake you, it's just…" I step forward, not taking my eyes off her, her lips, the tiny traces of freckles that dot her nose. I'm not sure how to tell her. Tell

her that I love her. That I know it for real now. That I want to be with

her forever and ever.

But I know I have to.

"Why do you love me?" I say instead, taking a deep breath

and watching her closely.

"What?"

"Why. Do. You. Love. Me?"

Cat shakes her head. "West, no, c'mon, we agreed to forget—

"

"Cat," I say. "Please just answer me." I grit my teeth. "Why do

you love me?"

"You really want to know?"

"I do."

She sighs. Turns. Looks at me. Her eyes linger on mine for the longest time before she says anything, taking me in, studying me. She's so beautiful, I realize, as the moonlight pours down on her. Perfect even though she just rolled out of bed—perfect *to me.*

I love her. I need her. We know each other inside and out, and she is my everything. She has been my everything since the beginning.

"I love you, West Ryder," Cat finally says, "because you're you. Because you're smart and funny and weird and so goddamn charming"—she smiles distantly—"and you aren't afraid to be *you.* I love you because we mesh, because you're weird and I'm weird and we're all weird together. When I'm around you I can't stop smiling and yeah, that's incredibly cheesy, but it is entirely true. I love you because I feel lonely when I'm not talking to you, not with you. I love you, West, because you are the one for me."

She stops then, draws in another breath, and steps closer to me. It's only a fraction of a movement, but it makes my heart skip a beat.

Her words seem to echo throughout the neighborhood. *I love you because you're you.*

"And you, West? Why are you asking this?" She says it so carefully it's like she's testing a frozen pond to make sure it supports her weight.

I give a little half-smile. "Can't a guy ask a question without ulterior motives?"

"Some guys, maybe. But you sure can't. I know you too well for that."

There's a long pause, and I can't stop staring at her. I feel so invincible now, because I love her and I finally, finally know it. I don't know how to tell it to her, to possibly put all she means to me into words. I can't, though. Words can't ever express how important Cat is to me, or how much I love her. "You know," I say quietly, "how every winter that creek down the street would freeze? And you'd always race down to it and when it was solid enough to walk on, you'd get all agitated? Well, I remember asking you what was wrong, because we could play on the ice and wasn't that a good thing? But you just shook your head like you knew something I didn't, and you told me that was the problem."

"It makes no sense, yeah," she says, looking at me uncertainly. "But I was eight."

I step forward again. I notice how her lips curl at my movement, how her eyes light up for the tiniest instant. "I know it makes no sense," I whisper. "But you and the creek…. It's the same as here. With me and you."

"Huh?"

I don't answer her this time. I squeeze my eyes shut, willing myself to tell her.

"What's the matter, West?" I open my eyes. Cat's are locked on mine, and she looks a mix between worry and a growing sense of curiosity.

"The matter? This is the matter. *All* of this. I'm frickin' in love with my best friend. I'm..." I take a deep breath and all of a sudden, it hits me. Just like that. "I'm in love with you, Cat," I whisper. "And it's like the creek because that's the problem: that I'm in love with you."

As soon as the words tumble out of my mouth, Cat's face lights up, and I see her suppressing a smile. She moves even closer to me now, her hips touching mine, and I feel her warmth against my body, her hands flickering, just slightly, back and forth and back and forth at her side. She's so close I could give in to temptation right now and touch her, kiss her, get lost in her closeness and her love.

I hold back.

Barely.

Finally, Cat opens her mouth to speak. I'm afraid she's going to say something scolding, or disappointed, or whatever the hell they say on TV when a character tells another character he loves her, but instead Cat just smiles. "You are so weird," she says simply.

My stomach tightens. "Yes?"

She doesn't respond. Instead, she reaches a hand out. I don't move as she traces the side of my face, my cheek, my smile with her fingers. My whole body tingles at her touch, and I just look at her, breathing in, breathing out. I feel so tight, and every single muscle in my body freezes up the instant her skin connects with mine. In that instant, all I want is for her to keep going, to keep touching me, to hold me, just hold me, until the world melts away. "Tomorrow is my birthday," she says.

"Yeah. I know."

She stops tracing, but her finger does not leave my skin. I'm so aware of her touch, of her closeness to me. I smell her vanilla shampoo, hear each of her soft, satisfied breaths. "My seventeenth birthday."

"I know…"

She glances up at me, her eyes now leveling with mine. They look so serious, like one touch will shatter them.

"Seventeen and in love," she says so softly I swear she's talking to herself. She sighs, and I can't move, can't look away from Cat. She keeps standing there, not moving, and all I want is for her to kiss me, to hold me, to never let go. My body wants it so badly that it both terrifies and exhilarates me, that I realize both her warmth and her lips are what I've been waiting for this whole time. She's my best friend and look where we are. Here. At midnight. Wanting each other. *Needing* each other.

But as I look into her eyes, as I remember all the time we've held hands and laughed and smiled like it was nothing, like we didn't care and didn't *want* to care, it doesn't even matter to me.

Because I love her.

"You know what would be a good birthday present?" she says finally, and presses her side to mine.

Now my smile really grows, and I inch my side closer to hers, my mouth hovering an inch away from her lips. "I think I do," I whisper.

"Then do it. Kiss me."

My throat catches at her words. I mean, I knew what she was getting at, but it still paralyzes me to hear her say it. At first, I don't know what to do, don't know whether kissing her is worth it, but my body answers for me.

I lean in. She's right there in front of me, her eyes closed, her lips outstretched. Waiting.

And I start to do it—to kiss her. I really do. But I hesitate there, my lips so close to hers, and all of a sudden the fear takes over. I pull back, shaking my head and hating myself. "I love you, Cat," I say softly, shifting my gaze to my feet, "and I realize now that I have all along. But I'm scared, scared of us. What if we do this and it doesn't work out? What if it makes us split apart? What if I can never be normal with you again, talk to you, laugh with you?"

She grabs my hand and pulls me closer. My skin tingles at her touch, and it feels so good, so right, when her skin brushes against mine. "It's supposed to be scary," she whispers, and I'm consciously aware of how close we are together. Our mouths hover there, a millimeter apart, and all I want is to man up and just fucking kiss her already. Her hand moves up and down my arm, and she smiles at me, a distant, sad smile. "And it's supposed to hurt. It's scary because it matters, West. I don't know what's going to happen to us myself, and the risk is just as terrifying to me. For all we know we're about to get fucked and tomorrow this will all end. But I'm not going to live my life thinking about what could have been. I'm not going to stop loving you, either. So yeah, if this doesn't work out, I will be crushed for the rest of my life. But I'm not going to say I didn't go down without a fight. I'm not going to say I didn't risk it. And the beauty of this risk, West Ryder," she says, pressing her stomach to mine, "is that no matter what, it will work out, because I will have spent time loving you." Then, she stops. Looks at me. My whole body trembles and I can't help but laugh a little. I feel so overcome I'm also convinced I'm going to cry. Cat's whole face seems to brighten at that, lips curling into a small smile, and I reach out and touch her face. Then, slowly, I run my finger up and down her cheek. I shudder, because it feels so good, and I realize how much I want to lean in and kiss her right then. She doesn't move, though, just stays all tense and stares right into my eyes, smiling a little. I can feel the tension in her body, the slight tremble of her lips, and all I want is to keep on going.

"I'm scared too, you know," she breathes, and her lips just linger there, in front of me, "but I'm ready to risk it because I know, deep down, that no matter what, I won't stop loving you."

All air seems to leave my body at once. Slowly, I drop my hand from her face and tilt my mouth just a fraction of an inch to the side. Something crosses her face then—a flicker of a smile, I think, because then I find myself smiling, too.

I lean in before I know what I'm doing. I move forward a little, then hesitate and pull back. My heart is racing in my chest as I watch her, and I swear by the glimmer in her eyes, hers is too. For a long moment, I just look at her and she back at me, each of us wondering who will be the one to seal the deal.

Then, I take a deep breath, and I lean in ever so slightly.

I don't realize my lips are pressed against hers until I feel a shock of emotion throughout my body, then the warmth of her lips touching mine. Cat wraps her arm around my neck and I hold my hands, so delicately, to her cheeks. She smiles through the kiss, gasps for air, then kisses me harder and harder. Our lips move perfectly in sync, touching and moving and craving more and more. It feels so right, though, and as she leans back against the door I keep kissing and kissing her. I can't stop. My whole body is buzzing with emotion and energy, and suddenly, it feels like I was destined to be here, with Cat, all along. Like this moment, this one kiss, has been years in the making.

And as I hold her there, our lips locked, I believe it.

There's a single breathless moment as we pull away from each other where we both just stare into each other's eyes, panting, our minds racing together to piece together what the hell just happened. My ears are ringing and my skin feels hot and my lips crave more of her touch, her kiss, but I also can't turn away from her. I don't *want* to turn away from her.

"This," Cat finally whispers, her blue eyes melting into mine, "calls for some celebratory ice cream."

Chapter 18

I don't go home that night.

Cat says her parents are away on another business trip and since we're both too tired and smiley to want to leave each other's side, she tells me to stay here for the night. With her. I don't even think about it before agreeing.

She gets out a sleeping bag for me, spreads it out in the corner of her room, and I take off my shirt and stretch across it as she climbs into her own bed. I watch as she covers herself with an array of blankets, smiling a little. I imagine what it would be like to lie there with her, to feel her heat, her body, her skin against mine. To just hold her and never, ever let go.

One day, I tell myself, I will get there.

Cat and I stay up late, just lying in our respective beds and laughing and talking with each other. We don't talk about what just happened, though. Not about the kiss, not about any of this. Instead, we spend our time discussing Switzerland politics, mostly about the political situation with Switzerland chocolate and how we might go about buying some more.

"Night, West," Cat says after a while, when the conversation dies down.

"Night, Cat," I say back. She winks at me. Then, she turns off the light and we're flooded in darkness.

I close my eyes, but I don't sleep. I mean, I try to, but all I can think about is the kiss and about Cat, now so close to me. She falls asleep quickly, and eventually I just lie there, listening to each of her soft breaths. I let myself smile. It's so peaceful—warm and cozy and peaceful—knowing she's at my side.

Even though we're separated by five feet of space, the possibilities with Cat and me race through my brain all night long. And I don't want them to stop, either.

The next morning, I get up early and make Cat an egg sandwich, which is complete with way too much bacon. I set it out for her, turn off the stove, sit on a chair in the kitchen, and wait for her to come down. She's still wearing her pajamas when she finally stumbles down the stairs, yawning and smiling at the same time.

"Hey," she says and slides into a seat at the table beside me. "Nice shirt," she adds, and I glance down at my bare stomach. I'm wearing nothing but my red-checkered boxers.

"I thought you might like that."

"Oh, believe me, I do," she says, pouring herself an orange juice.

The morning air cools my body as I reheat the eggs, then scrape them back off the pan and onto a fresh plate. Then, I put halves of an English muffin on either side of the egg, wrap it in bacon and cheese, and slide the plate across the counter over to her.

She sniffs it and smiles. "Extra bacon?"

"Of course."

"You know me so well."

I grin. I grab the little remaining bits of egg, scoop it into my own plate, and join Cat at the table. She squeezes my hand, and another string of warmth goes through me. "Thanks for breakfast," Cat says. "You're almost a better cook than *I* am."

"Always, Red Velvet," I say. "Always.

We spend the rest of the morning gossiping, debating which food item is the most superior (ice cream, duh), and Cat makes a "why did the chicken cross the road?" joke that causes me to laugh before she even says the joke, because something about the fact that a chicken would cross a road for a real purpose in the first place is so hilarious to me. Eventually, when we're both finished with breakfast and I've cleared the plates, the morning melts into turning on the local news and making fun of as many things about it as possible. It's a perfect Saturday, really, and I don't think I've ever smiled more.

She's mine now, and I'm hers, and something about that makes me feel so utterly invincible.

"So Cat," I say finally, standing on the other side of the counter and turning to her. "Today is your birthday, and we must celebrate it like true dorks. Besides, that is, talking to this hot shirtless stranger who has made you breakfast."

She rolls her eyes. "And where *is* this hot stranger? I'm not seeing him…"

I snort at that, then proceed to shoot her a look. She holds up her hands in defense. "Hey man," she says. "I'm just speaking the truth."

"Hater."

"Liar."

"So," I say, leaning toward her from across the counter. "Shall we celebrate your birthday with ice cream?"

"OH MY GOD YESSSS! ICE CREEEAAAM!" She stands up on the counter and starts shouting at me.

I hide my smile. "I take it you want ice cream?"

"Oh yes, West Ryder, I *so* do."

"Then that's where we'll celebrate your birthday."

"Good. Feel free to invite that hot shirtless stranger as well."

"I will," I say, leaning in to kiss her on the cheek. I shiver at the touch of her skin, but it's a good kind of shiver. A *happy* shiver. "Now if you'll excuse me," I say, and start heading upstairs to get a shirt and the rest of my things, "I should go. We'll go later?"

"Yeah, okay," she says, and I run up the stairs.

"Hey, West?" Cat calls when I come back down, opening the front door.

"Yeah?"

"You're the best birthday present anyone can ask for," she says.

I only smile at her, step through the door, and walk out. "I could say the same about you."

**

Dad is waiting by the door when I come home. His arms are folded, and the instant I lay eyes on him, my grin fades. For a second, as I stop in front of him, I think he's going to scream at me for leaving for the night. But he doesn't.

"Dad, look, I'm sorry—" I mumble as I step inside, preparing for another drunken rage. "I should've told you I was leaving, but please don't—"

He stops me, holds up a finger, and shakes his head. "It's okay," he says softly, in a way that almost sounds like he... cares?

I freeze, surprised. This is totally strange. But he *has* to be pretending again, because my father does not care. Not anymore.

"I didn't come here to yell at you," he continues. "I came to give you this."

I watch him carefully as he holds out his hand, offering me a glass bird of some sort.

I frown at him, trying to determine what exactly he's trying to pull on me this time. "What is this?" I don't mean to say it so bluntly, but it comes out of my mouth before I can stop it. I'm not used to having much of a filter around my dad, I guess.

He smiles vaguely. "This," he says, "is a phoenix pendant. It was your mother's. I gave it to her on our first date."

"Oh," I say. My heart sinks a little, and I feel suddenly uncomfortable talking to him, like I have to get the hell out of there right now. I don't want to talk to my dad, especially not about Mom, especially not after all this time. So I sigh and look past him into the hallway, debating whether it would be worth it to slip under his arm and run straight to my room without responding. I decide to wait it through.

"'Oh' is right," Dad says, taking a breath. "I even remember when I first gave that to her. I said something entirely cheesy and stupid when I handed it to her. I think I told her that phoenixes matter because they rise from the ashes, so when time gets tough I wanted her to wear this to remind herself to be the phoenix—and to rise above the ashes. I know, I was such a geek, but you know what she did when I told her that?"

"What?" I say, not really caring. Whatever gets me away from here and back to my room thinking about Cat fastest works for me.

"She laughed at me," Dad says. He sighs at the memory, a glimmer of happiness flickering across his lips. "But she still took it. She wore it as a necklace but tucked it under her shirt, and it was like a secret glass bird only the two of us knew about. It was nice, I guess. Nice to have something between us." He hands me the phoenix. "Take it, West. It's yours."

I hesitate. "Why are you giving me this?" I say, knowing there's got to be a catch, especially because it's Dad. And anyway, what father gives his son jewelry? Maybe this phoenix has the world's tiniest bomb or something attached to it? I wouldn't be surprised, honestly.

"To give to that special someone, of course."

My stomach clenches. "What are you talking about?"

"If I can't tell when my own son is in love, I'm a horrible father." He laughs to himself, and I feel the heat creep into my cheeks. Vaguely, I wonder if he knows about Cat, if even he has known how in love with her I was even before I did. We're silent for a long while, though, and I don't know what to say. This is all too weird.

Finally, I pocket the phoenix.

"Thanks," I mumble and start to head to the stairs, to just get away from this strangeness, but his voice, echoing through the hall, stops me. "I watched your vlog," he says quietly, not meeting my gaze. His eyes look sad, his face worn and empty of emotion.

My legs freeze up. "What?" Dad isn't supposed to know about my vlog. *No one* but Mom is supposed to know.

"I watch all your vlogs, West."

"But how… how do you know about those?"

He shakes his head. "I'm a bad father, West, but I'm not an idiot."

I blush. Hard.

"And," he continues, "I'm sorry. I was an asshole. I've *been* an asshole for a year now, and I wasn't there for you when you needed it most." He takes a step closer to me, and I feel oddly light-headed. He sounds so sincere, so much that it hurts. I swallow hard, choking back a tear. "I'm… trying to quit, quit drinking and being so horrible," he says. "I want to change. To work. To be a dad again. A good dad. A real dad. *Your* dad, West. I want to be *your* dad." He takes a deep breath, his gray eyes studying me. "And I want to know… will you ever forgive me?"

My skin crawls, and my heart starts racing all over again. He sounds so serious, so genuine, so unlike himself... He isn't making this all up, and I know it instantly by the way his eyes watch me. He's being serious. For once, he wants to change. "You're... you're for real?" I ask, realizing it's true but not wanting to face the inevitable.

"I am," Dad says, nodding.

I clench my jaw. Then, I look at him, at his small smile, his sober expression. He looks so cleaned up, like a whole new person now, like he really is ready to change.

I look into his eyes, which glimmer with the faintest shreds of hope. *Hope.* He has hope. Maybe hope that he'll get better, maybe that he'll fix his mistakes and become a decent person, or maybe hope that I'll let him back in. For an instant, I am tempted to do it—to forgive him. It would be so easy and it might even lift a weight off my chest. But as I study him, his jaw tightening harder and harder, I know I won't. I *can't.* I don't care whether he is ready to change. He's still the same father who killed my mother and who treated me, and her,

like shit for a year. I can't ever forgive him for that.

"No," I finally whisper, my hands shaking. "I'm sorry, but I

can't."

Chapter 19

Later that day, I wait in front of the ice cream shop for Cat to arrive. It's 2:00 in the afternoon, and I stand there, sun on my back, holding my phone and aimlessly refreshing my vlog page. I texted Cat saying to meet me here for her "birthday party," which, as she correctly pointed out, is really just an excuse for me to eat more ice cream. A damn fine one at that, I might add.

Under my arm I hold the cake I made for her last night, which is now complete with the pictures of her and me I pulled out. I look around for Cat, for her face, her hair, her smile—because seeing her, no matter what, always seems to make my day brighter. She isn't there, though, and I go back to my phone. People rush by all around me, gossiping and discussing the latest clothing sales and aimlessly swinging their shopping bags as they push past me. Cars rumble by, and the air smells like a mixture of cigarettes and exhaust. Not exactly the most pleasant scent.

But as I move closer to *The Icecreamery*, the wonderful smell of vanilla ice cream fills my nose. My stomach growls. I need that ice cream.

After a minute, my mind drifts to thinking about Dad and what he said. A part of me feels guilty for turning him down because I know in my heart that he really is trying, but I just can't let him off like that, like nothing happened. He made my life miserable for over a year and even though he's changing, I can't just forgive him all of a sudden. I can't let him off the hook so easily. Somehow, it doesn't feel right, especially not after what he did to Mom.

Maybe, one day, I'll forgive him. But he'll have to work for it.

I sigh and refresh my phone again. This time, a notification shows—a new comment on my vlog. I frown. It's from... HarperLikesPizza?

Wait...

But Harper is…

…fake…

Right?

Immediately, I scroll over to the comment, my throat catching, wondering what exactly is going on. When I read over the comment, a breath of relief escapes me. "It's time to move on from me, O' Illustrious Sam Green," it reads. "I hear there's this hot Cat girl waiting for you in the ice cream shop behind you, too… AND it's her birthday. You should totally check her out. In fact, she's so amazing that one could make the argument that she *is* me."

I let out a little smile. Cat seriously got me there. I check the time—2:02. Right when Harper always comments. So I let my cheekbones appear, mumble "Goodbye, Harper," shut my phone, and turn around.

I have a girlfriend to meet.

Cat waves to me through *The Icecreamery* window, and I jog in after her. Cool air blasts me as I step into the shop, and I hear the familiar hum of freezers everywhere. The wondrous scent of ice cream surrounds me as I walk over to Cat, who is seated in the corner.

The place is quiet for once, with only two squealing toddlers and their mom this time, both on the opposite side of the room. The rest of the shop is just Cat and me.

"Are you Cat, the hot girl I heard I should meet?" I say to her as I approach.

"That I am." She gets to her feet and touches my shoulder with her hand. "Are you ready for the ice cream of a lifetime, oh wonderfully charismatic stranger?"

"Ummmmm hell yes."

I take her hand then, and we walk over to the cashier, laughing at each other's stupidity. "Can I help you?" the same cashier from before asks, recognizing us. I don't mean to brag, of course, but we're pretty damn popular in the world of children's ice cream.

I glance at Cat, who squeezes my hand, and I turn back to the cashier. "Boy could you, Sharon…"

"I'm well aware, West," Sharon responds, suppressing a little smile.

I quirk my eyebrow and scan the freezer, as if it's actually a possibility that I'll choose a different ice cream flavor than always, even though we all know it isn't.

"I will have your finest vanilla ice cream," I say at last. "With sprinkles and a cherry and in a kiddy cone, please."

"And what kind of sprinkles would you like, sir?" she says just to get me going. I can't help but notice the irony of her calling a sixteen-year-old boy who is ordering a rainbow-sprinkled vanilla ice cream in a kiddy cone "sir." But I like it anyway.

"Rainbow sprinkles. They are what make the world go 'round. Literally."

"I'm well aware. A world without rainbow sprinkles is a world without happiness."

"Yes!" I say too loudly. Then I turn to Cat. "See, Red Velvet? *Someone* who gets me!"

Cat rolls her eyes.

"And you?" Sharon asks Cat.

"The same thing," she says, "but with chocolate sprinkles, please." She shoots me a look.

"Wow," I say, feigning a gasp. "No rainbow sprinkles? Some nerve you have there, woman."

She melodramatically tosses her hair. "I guess you could see I'm feeling gutsy today."

"Oh really? Is that hot shirtless stranger rubbing off on you?" I ask.

"Maybe so."

Once the ice cream is done, we pay Sharon, thank her for her "continued support in the children's ice cream industry," grab our cones, and sit down. This time, though, Cat does not sit opposite me. She pulls up a chair directly next to mine, nudges my shoulder, and it feels so good to be this close to her.

"Whatcha got there?" Cat says, pointing at the wrapped-up cake under my arm.

"Oh, just the greatest birthday present in the history of the world. No bigs."

"For me?" she asks, batting her eyelashes.

"No, no, of course not. I'm just holding it for a friend."

She rolls her eyes. "One day, I'm going to be damned for falling in love with someone so weird."

"And thank god this is not that day." I slide the present over to her across the table. "Open it," I say.

"Are you sure?"

"Yes. As long as you promise to prepare for badassery."

Cat laughs a little. "I promise."

Then, she glances down, tears off the bow, rips apart the striped Harry Potter wrapping paper, and slowly lifts the tinfoil underneath to reveal a giant, chocolate-gummy-worm-Oreo cake with old pictures of us forming a fence around the side.

She covers her mouth with her hand. "West, this is perfect," she whispers and just stares at the gift. "You are an effing fantastic cook." She touches her finger to the first photograph, then sifts through all twelve, her mouth curling into a huge grin and her eyes so bright it makes my whole body come to life.

"Oh, I could so kiss you right now," she continues. Then, she leans closer. "You know. That doesn't sound like such a bad idea after all... shall we?"

A flicker of a smile crosses my lips. "Nuh-uh-uh! Not yet."

"Why not?" she says, clearly amused.

"Because first, ICE CREAM EATING CONTEST!"

Cat shoots me a look. "Fine. But you're so going down, Ryder."

"Oh, Red Velvet, we'll see about that," I say, giving her my best intimidation face, in which I wave my hand in front of my eyes like I've seen wrestlers do. It fails miserably, and she starts cracking up.

"Oh yeah?" she says.

"Oh yeah."

"Then let's do this."

"Yes. Let's."

We grab our ice creams at almost the exact same time.

"Ready," she says, and it's a total déjà vu moment.

"Set," I say.

We smile at each other, our eyes locking, leaning toward our ice creams. "GO!!!!!!!!!!"

Immediately, I pounce on the ice cream and eat it so fast my teeth seem to freeze from its coldness. Cat and I get weird looks from all around us, but it's not like we even care. I keep eating and eating, letting the cool ice cream slide down my throat, watching Cat shove the cone literally *at* her face, and I find myself suppressing a laugh. Finally, when I pull away from the ice cream, it's just the cherry left, along with a few splotches of ice cream on the table. Cat has already finished, though, and I laugh when I see the vanilla still smeared across her lips.

She shoots me a look. "I guess I win that," she says.

"There are no victors here," I say. "Only me and everyone else."

There's a pause, and we both just sit there, squeezing each other's hands and smiling.

"You know," Cat says after a few minutes, "it's funny how love is so complicated and yet sometimes, it's as simple as your vlog."

"How so?" I ask, frowning. "Please don't get overly-sentimental on me, Red Velvet."

She rolls her eyes. "Well, sometimes love is right in front of you the whole time, even if you don't realize it. And, like your vlog, all you have to do is click to subscribe."

I raise my eyebrow. "That's a terrible a metaphor."

She laughs. "Dude, I know. I have nothing to say, okay!"

She sighs, and then I look at her—really look at her. She is glowing, like seriously glowing. Her smile makes *me* smile, her long red hair always manages to take my breath away, and her vanilla ice cream-covered lips just prove to me what a fantastically awesome dork she is.

And I love her.

I really do.

"So about that kiss…?" Cat whispers.

I smile. "Yes," I breathe, "I'm ready." Then, I lean in, and I kiss the ice cream off her lips.

Epilogue

Cat and I aren't married now. We don't have kids, a happy family, a perfect life. But one thing we do have is each other—and that's something that will never, ever leave us. As of yesterday we've been dating for six months, and so Cat and I decided the milestone called for a celebration. So we came here.

I haven't posted a vlog in months. I've been too busy thinking about Cat to be funny or at all interesting, really. My last vlog post, after the one where I spilled my thoughts about Cat and my dad to the camera, was with Cat—a victory vlog, you can call it—and we laughed and flirted and were entirely awkward the whole time. It was probably the worst video I've ever filmed, with the only point to "show off how happy I am," but I don't even care, because now things are different.

Now I'm in love.

I sigh. Just thinking about Cat brings a smile to my lips. Trust me, that is a *hell* of a lot of smiles.

I sit on the grass next to the driveway as Cat pulls in with her car. A slight breeze ruffles my hair as I look out at the ocean stretching in front of me, off into the distance. Seagulls fly everywhere above us, squawking and diving for clams or whatever, and I listen to the rhythmic crashing of waves onto the sand, the distant laughs of neighbors on their own beaches, and the rumble of trucks driving by.

When Cat steps out of her car, I turn my head to her, shielding the sun with my left hand, and smiling.

"Hey you," I say as she approaches. Then, I nod to the car. It's sleek and slim with perfect, glossy-red paint, and it looks brand new, even though it's ten years old. "Your dad's Mercedes is also looking pretttty freaking nice. You did an awesome job fixing it."

She sits down next to me, smiling too. "You mean *we* did an awesome job fixing it."

I hold up my hands. "Can't argue with that! I'm just glad we were finally able to use it."

"Me too," she says, and then, as I look at her, I can't help but put my arm around her. She leans her head into my shoulder and, with the wind whipping against us, we stare out at the horizon and the water and sand of the beach below.

"It's beautiful," I breathe, because as I take in my surroundings I realize that it really is just that: beautiful. But even more beautiful than the beach is Cat and the feeling she gives me. With my arm around her it's like I'm omnipotent, like her warmth is my Kryptonite.

"It is." I follow her gaze to the giant, all-wood beach house to our right. "And that, West Ryder, is the holy grail of beach houses. My grandfather was a genius when it came to buying real estate."

"For sure. This is going to be a perfect week away from the rest of the world. Just you and me," I whisper.

She nods. "I always told you that when I fixed up that Mercedes, I'd take the boy of my dreams here." She turns to me, her blue eyes sparkling. "And I was right."

Then, she leans in, and with the sun shining down on our backs, our lips lock.

Acknowledgements

As I write these acknowledgements, I still can't believe that this is really happening. (I'm not dreaming this all up, right? My book is seriously being published?)

I would not be here today without my fabulous critique partners Joy and Stephanie. Thank you for listening to my pointless rants and for making me a better writer. And to AJOMA, my writer's group, who may or may not ever read this—you guys seriously rock my world. I am so appreciative of the random late-night chats, the weirdness, and the constant support. I'd be lost without all you.

I would also like to thank Tristina Wright and Allie Brennan for beta-reading this book on a moment's notice and for providing such insightful feedback. *Click* could not have happened without you. Much love, as well, to B Design, for taking my very rough vision of a book cover and turning it into something so utterly perfect. I could not have asked for a better design.

To bloggers Anna Reads Romance, Just A Book Lover, Candy Coated Book Blog, I Heart Books, Books Over Boys, Can't Read Just One, and to authors Helen Boswell, Alessandra Thomas, Laura Howard, Katy Evans, Priya Kanaparti, Leigh Ann Kopans, Adriane Boyd, Cora Carmack, Beth Michele, and all of the other amazing bloggers and authors who have helped me along the way —your love and support has made me feel so much more confident in this decision. Thank you.

I am also eternally grateful for John Green, Colleen Hoover, and the other YA and NA authors out there whose books and absolutely amazing characters have given me the courage to publish my own.

Last of all, I want to thank everyone who reads *Click To Subscribe*. Whether you liked it or not it means so much to me that you gave this little story a chance.

About L.M. Augustine

L.M. Augustine is a YA romance author who is obsessed with writing about dorky teenagers, love, and happy endings. He currently lives in New England, where he spends far too much time reading books and screaming at his computer, and he believes that the solution to the world's problems can be found in chocolate cake. *Click To Subscribe* is his first novel, but it won't be his last. Feel free to follow his Facebook page, his Twitter account, and/or his blog for book news, random GIFs, and overall just plain strangeness.

P.S. I love my readers to death, so feel free to get in touch! I'll do my best to respond to all emails/tweets/FB posts ASAP.

CPSIA information can be obtained at www.ICGtesting.com
Printed in the USA
LVOW10s0105210813

348828LV00029B/2098/P